THE SIXTH BLOOD

WRITTEN & ILLUSTRATED BY

RYAN J. MURRELL

[Ryan J Murrell] [2023]

All rights reserved. No part of this novella, "The Sixth Blood," may be reproduced, distributed, or transmitted in any form or by any means, including photocopying, recording, or other electronic or mechanical methods, without the prior written permission of the publisher, except in the case of brief quotations embodied in critical reviews and certain other noncommercial uses permitted by copyright law.

This is a work of fiction. Names, characters, places, and incidents are either products of the author's imagination or used fictitiously. Any resemblance to actual persons, living or dead, events, or locales is entirely coincidental.

For more information about the author and updates on "The Sixth Blood," please visit: [rycreates.net]

Thank you for respecting the author's work and intellectual property rights. Your support is greatly appreciated.

DEDICATED TO MY MOTHER
MICHELLE MURRELL, MY BIGGEST
SUPPORTER

PROLOGUE

The fading moonlight reflected against Resmé's silver hair as she stood over the towering cliff's edge, shimmering waves below crashing against the unmovable foot of stone. Her aged body stood tall and strong, despite the assaulting whirls of wind that threatened to carry her over the edge. Her fathomless gray eyes pierced through the darkness and over the restless water into the horizon – searching, waiting.

Suddenly sensing a presence behind her, Resmé's mouth curved into a slight smile.

"After all these years, I didn't believe you would come." she said solemnly, not turning her face away from the ocean.

"There wasn't much else of a choice in this matter, old friend." said the burly man, his hands burying deep inside the pockets of his long black trench coat.

Resmé turned to him, folding her arms gently. "There's always a choice, Horace. You made a choice to abandon us for decades without word…"

"-Please Resmé," he interrupted. "I'm aware that my actions weren't the most noble. Even still, there was no other way to locate what needed to be found."

She looked up into his saddened eyes for a moment, turning once more to the sea.

"The past remains the past. *I* of all people realize an eternity holds no place for bitterness. Even still, that isn't what I called you here for. "

Horace approached her side, his tall robust frame towering over her own.

"You've found him?"

She nodded slowly.

"It's been centuries since I've felt it *this* strong.

The time is growing near, faster than we can prepare I fear."

"What of the other bloodlines?

"I've been able to keep them hidden over the years, although they still only have the slightest grasp on the power they truly possess."

"-Making them the easiest of prey."

"Precisely, I'm afraid. Time doesn't allow us to search for every single remaining bloodline. The boy is our last hope in these final days."

"But his age Resmé ...so young to bear such a burden."

"I wish we had the luxury of waiting until he's fully matured, but that time has already passed. We're desperate, Horace. You understand that. If he isn't able to seal the barrier-" She held off the last words, knowing both she and Horace knew well the horrors that would come to pass.

Horace placed a steady hand on the older woman's shoulder. "He will," he assured her. "He must."

Resmé gently touched Horace's bearded face. "Your faith was always admirable to me, but it won't be enough to save this world. You must realize that countless lives of our people have already been lost."

Horace pushed her hand away.

"Of course I realize, better than anyone else could understand. What must be done couldn't be any clearer to me."

"You'll go to him then?"

"But why? You're much more...approachable than I."

"Because you were a great leader, Horace, and I believe you still can be. There's no one better to bring him to his full potential."

Horace ran his fingers through his gray-streaked brown curls, sighing deeply.

"Very well then. I'll do my duty to him in this short

time. But it will take protection from both of us to shield him from the Asdroth Core. They're fast approaching as I'm sure you can sense."

"It will take protection from both us and the remaining bloodlines to hold off all that is coming. I can only imagine what chaos an entire legion will unleash upon the world."

"That will never be found out." Horace interjected, his eyes gazing intently into the dark forest behind.

"The fate of our world will not fall upon this one, I swear. It will be saved."

Resmé's eyes fell, head nodding subtly, "Even if our lives are sacrificed."

Horace lifted her chin gently with a finger. "What more of a noble way to bring our eternity of existence to an end."

With that, he vanished into the whirling wind, the sensation of his touch still lingering on Resmé's face. She once again stood alone under the fading moon, eyes returning to the distant horizon as gentle rays of sunlight cut through the dark sky.

Chapter One

The pouring rain pelts against my attic window, strange shadows dancing along the walls as moonlight pierces through. With every crack of thunder and gust of wind, the entire house groans and sways, the aged wooden frame nearly bending past its breaking point. My eyes aren't able to shut for even a moment before the rumbling floorboards jostle me awake again.

I've been counting droplets of water leaking through cracks in the ceiling for hours now, hoping my mind wanders to any other thoughts aside from the assaulting storm. The unfortunate thing is, I don't have an overwhelming amount of comforting thoughts to turn to at the moment.

"Find the positives in everything" the voice of my school counselor echoes in my head. I suppose her

advice has helped a bit, maybe I haven't given it enough of a shot. For now, the weekly therapy sessions haven't exactly made happiness feel more attainable. There seems to be a cloud that lingers over my head after our discussions, a cloud even heavier than the ones pouring torrential rains down on us now.

It's taken years of reworking my inner dialogue to decide that I'm not "disturbed" or "peculiar" as my foster families claimed, even if isolated incidents in the past made it appear otherwise. My early years in the system were an exhausting rollercoaster. Unfamiliar families and houses every few seasons, constant relocation of schools. Worst of all were the quiet, lonely nights - and *the voices* that accompanied them.

Faint, ghostly voices that were distinctly separate from my own internal one. Whatever words they spoke were as clear as fogged-over glass, a wondering thought I couldn't fully grasp. I was only seven when they first appeared, and the fear surrounding them faded as they became constant. No different than white noise, or the background echoes of traffic.

The horror etched on my foster mother's face at my revelation hinted at a deeper, *unsettling* truth. This concerning discovery set in motion a series of transfers, each home presenting unique difficulties.

Every new family had their own worries, none involving actual menacing behavior on my part, although they would all claim otherwise to get me from under their roof. They were disturbed by something I couldn't understand, especially considering I stopped mentioning the voices all together. Sure, maybe I was a bit of an odd-ball kid, but the memories from those times glazed over gradually throughout the years.

As the voices vanished entirely just before the start of middle school, I sum them up to an overactive imagination, undoubtedly influenced by unstable living conditions.

Ten years later, I'm sleeping in a freezing attic on a frameless mattress, covered only by a thin quilt that won't reach past my ankles. The Dunkles insist that simple requests for comfort are simply too much of a burden, a philosophy they've fully embraced over the last three years I've been fostered under them.

I grip the mattress underneath me as another strong gust of wind assaults the small room once again. The alarm clock sitting on the floor beside my mattress reads ten o'clock, although I know it's an hour behind. An eternity before sunrise.

A violent growling in my stomach distracts me momentarily from the storm; the result of eating only two dry peanut butter sandwiches last night. If I hadn't saved them from school lunch yesterday, I would've gone to sleep even hungrier than now. Meanwhile, the refrigerator downstairs is filled with leftovers of the steak and potato dinner the Dunkles enjoyed earlier tonight. After another glance at the clock, I step onto the cold, splintered wooden floors, pulling the quilt tightly around my shoulders.

I walk softly over to the small latch door that separates the attic from the rest of the house, careful to avoid creaking floor boards. Descending the steep narrow steps, I can already feel warmth creeping up to meet my chilled skin.

Along the right side of the short hallway is the open door to Mrs. and Mr. Dunkles' bedroom. Forceful snoring and slurred speech spill out of it and throughout the entire house. Claretta has the disturbing habit of fussing in her sleep, occasionally even acting out violently. It amazes me that her husband hasn't taken a punch or two just yet.

Further down the hall, there's a mirror hanging on the wall just before the stairs leading to the first level of the house. As I gaze at my exhausted reflection, I tussle the tight brown curls on my head to lessen the unkemptness. Sighing deeply, I realize that I've never been able to look into the mirror without tearing myself apart in some way. Whether it's my slender shoulders, the absence of facial hair, or my stature seemingly at odds with my age. Everything together illustrates a picture that defines what people know and think about Ethan Bennett when they see his shell.

Honestly, my name stands as the only thing I wouldn't change about myself; the sole remnant of a past I never knew—a past that held parents, a family, and a home. My name represents my unknown better half that I'm hoping still exists.

Mr. Dunkles' snores drown out my creaking footsteps, thankfully. A lightning flash illuminates the kitchen as I reach downstairs, revealing piles of unwashed dishes and filthy appliances throughout. The lingering smell of grease and spoiled food permeates the entire lower level, I'm almost grateful that I'm forbidden to step foot in here on a regular basis.

As I open the refrigerator door, the bright light blinds me for a moment. Carefully reaching around the half empty beer bottles and expired milk carton, I remove the saran-wrapped leftover steak. Struggling to keep my mouth from watering, I remove the plastic and let the delicious smell reach up to my nose. I'll have to eat it cold; the sound of the microwave would be an unnecessary risk.

Taking one of the only clean knives from the silverware drawer, I carefully attempt to trim around the meat inconspicuously. The taste of the beef only intensifies my stomach rumblings. It's surprising that the Dunkles could afford it, given that neither holds a steady job, opting instead to recline in the house, immersed in their own idleness. The only money they have coming in is what they receive for supposedly taking care of me for the past three years, right along with disability checks for ailments that I've never seen evidence of. I painfully place the plastic back over the plate of meat, turning to set it back into the refrigerator.

The kitchen light flickers on abruptly. Startled, I nearly drop the plate as I turn to see who's flipped the switch.

In the doorway stands the Dunkles' Sasquatch of a son, a smug toothy grin stretched along his face. Although we're just about the same age, Declan stands a foot taller than me, and his weight nearly twice my own. His dirty blond hair is smeared greasily against his forehead, eyes red with fatigue. I've never figured out how someone of his size can move around the house so silently, always finding some opportunity to sneak up on me.

"So, you're helping yourself to our stuff now, huh?" he sneers, his brawny arms folded defiantly across his chest.

"I was hungry, that's all. I barely touched it," I reply defensively, my hand clenched in a tight fist.

"Doesn't matter how much you ate. Stealing is stealing." He steps closer to me, near enough that I can smell the stench of his breath.

17

"You and I both know my parents will kick you back into the streets where you belong any day now. All I have to do is give them a reason."

"Well, that would be terrible," I grin, "There's nothin' I love more than living with the Two Stooges and their delinquent son."

The moment the words leave my mouth, I feel a brutal shove bash me against the nearby edge of the kitchen sink behind.

"Watch your mouth!" Declan hisses through clenched teeth, lurching forward to grab me up by my T-shirt. My hip throbs in pain from the contact on the granite surface, but anger overpowers the feeling entirely.

Before my brain can fully register what I'm about to do, all I can feel is the contact of my clenched fist colliding into his pudgy jaw. He crumbles backward into the countertop behind him, elbow knocking over a small stack of dirty porcelain plates. Not long after they crash to the floor, the sound of heavy footsteps descends hurriedly down the stairs.

As Mrs. Dunkle enters the kitchen, her gaze shifts from her son writhing in pain on the floor, up to meet my eyes, her sunken face reddening with anger. I could almost laugh at the combination of her ferocity joined with a frilly nightgown and slippers. The rollers in her thin black hair nearly fall loose as her head shakes with outrage.

"This is the last straw you evil brat!" she seethes, kneeling by her weeping son.

Declan releases his reddening jaw. "I caught him tryin' to steal food from us, then he just hit me ma'."

My fist clenches tightly once more, the urge to pummel both of them tugging at my chest. Yet, I stay still, silent. Nothing I say ever makes any kind of difference; it never does. There's another pair of heavy footsteps sounding from the upper level as Harold pounds down the stairs and into the kitchen. The sight of him in his bathrobe that barely conceals his boxers and beer belly underneath is nauseating.

His twisted face mirrors the same reddish color as Mrs. Dunkle's as he takes in the situation. I tune out the exaggerated details that Declan sobs to his father in a childish voice, staring down at the worn wooden floors beneath my bare feet. Amidst all this nonsense, I hadn't noticed that the storm has calmed somewhat. Outside the kitchen window, I see the trees have stopped erratically swaying in the wind.

I'm jolted back to reality as I see Harold stomp towards me, reaching forward to snatch me by the ear. The sudden pain forces a yell from me as he drags me across the kitchen floor.

"If you think you can just do whatever the hell you want in my house you got another thing comin' kid." He growls down at me, pulling me away from Claretta and Declan and out of the kitchen.

"I don't even know why we bother showing you a little bit of kindness-" he continues, dragging me as I stumble down the narrow hallway.

"Nothin' we give will get through that hard head of yours."

I try to wrench my ear free from his vice-like grip, searing in pain as his fingers tighten around it. As he swings open the front door to the house, a draft of brisk autumn air rushes in, the scent of rain-soaked earth filling my nose.

Before I can get my bearings, I find myself stumbling down the porch steps and onto the muddy ground, my bare feet slipping without traction as Mr. Dunkle continues to pull my ear behind him. Through the darkness, I can see that he's dragging me towards the cellar that lies to the side of the small brick house, its weathered exterior barely visible under the dim moonlight

"Please, I honestly didn't mean it!" my insides want to shout at him, but I refuse to give him the satisfaction of my pleading. As we reach the cellar, he reaches down to unfasten the rusted chains that hold the metal doors shut. The smell of gasoline and mildew pour out of the dark opening, forcing a cough from both of us.

"If some solitary confinement doesn't fix you up, I don't know what will." Harold spits, shoving me into the pitch blackness.

Quickly, he slams the doors shut, the sound of rattling chains following soon after. The suffocating darkness overwhelms all my senses, not even the slightest bit of moonlight seeping through the cracks of the stone walls. I close my eyes, although there's no difference whatsoever. It's a reassuring feeling somehow.

  Slowly, I edge my foot in the vicinity around me to assess the amount of space. I cringe as a thick spider web tangles around my toes, brushing it off frantically. Feeling a somewhat clear walkway to my right, I move into the small corner of the cellar, clearing away what feels like gardening tools and small stones. I sigh deeply, pulling my knees up to my chest.

"There's always something to be happy about." echoes my shrink's voice once again. I laugh silently, shaking my head. I'm drowning it feels like, sinking in my own thoughts that the universe had only dropped me accidentally on this earth.

  For once, could you make life just a little bearable? I ask the nothingness, halfheartedly hoping for just a little bit of good fortune considering my birthday is only minutes away. When the clock strikes twelve, it will be seventeen years since I was born, and anonymously released to a New Jersey orphanage soon after. Never did I receive any form of birthday wish from my foster families, but I don't suppose I could blame them. They were too preoccupied trying to decipher what was wrong with the "peculiar boy" residing in their home.

    The darkness around me deepens, if that's even possible. As chilled air pricks my bare arms and legs, I attempt to heat my numb hands by blowing warm air into them. My eyes remain closed, the only way I know to protect myself from the unknowns of the darkness.

    Even as a small child, no fear pressed on me as heavily as that of the dark. I always sensed a presence in the shadows, distinct from the voices, a feeling I couldn't explain then and struggle to understand even now. A shadowy abyss that swallowed me whole, leaving no hope of returning to the surface.

    My eyes squeeze even tighter, urging the darkness in my mind away with every ounce of strength, trying to grasp the brightest memory hidden in my obscured past. What I can finally cling onto is the prospect of some kind of hope, a hope that the shadows seemingly attached to my life will dissolve in the light that I'm summoning into existence.

Suddenly, the chilled air around me becomes warm against my skin. Through my closed eyelids, a small glint of light reaches my eyes. I open them slowly and see something completely startling. A few feet in front of me is a small blur of light that I initially believe to be a lightbulb. As it begins to grow, however, I realize it's not like anything I've ever seen.

Tongues of light spread from the blur as it forms into the shape of a distorted glowing orb, instantaneously forcing away the shadows around. My heart races as the light expands to the size of a beach ball, the tongues of luminescence reaching out just inches away from me. The golden glow envelops me entirely, warming me as it unveils every object and feature of the cellar.

With each heartbeat pounding in my chest, the light pulses, expanding until it's close enough that I can hear the faint hum radiating from it. I extend the palm of my hand as the light engulfs my body, a feeble attempt to push back the bewildering radiance.

Abruptly, it vanishes as mysteriously as it appeared, leaving the air vibrating with lingering warmth. The only sound is my heavy breath as darkness floods around me once again, the blinding light etching itself permanently in the pages of my memory.

CHAPTER TWO

The hours until sunrise pass by quickly as thoughts race frantically through my mind in the darkness. As the morning light filters into the cellar through the slit in the metal doors, my eyes remain fixed on the spot where the orb of light had appeared, a sense of disbelief lingering. Above all, fear courses through my entire body, a deep-down dread that the nightmarish episodes of "mental instability" I experienced as a child have returned with a vengeance.

As the cellar doors swing open and Harold allows me to step out from the darkness, I remain silent, walking stiffly toward the front of the crooked wooden house, ignoring the tyrannical gibberish he spews after me. I suppose it's around seven in the morning based on the amount of sunlight that is peaking over the horizon, Declan has probably left for school already. Not that Harold or Claretta would care if I miss the bus – they've shown time and again that my education and well-being are at the bottom of their priority list.

Climbing the creaking stairs, I wash away the grime in the small sink of the upstairs bathroom before returning to my chilled attic room. Dull morning light seeps through every crack in the wooden ceiling, creating streaks that cut through the dusty atmosphere. I fall face first onto my lumpy mattress, breathing out harshly.

"I'll just forget" I mutter to myself, echoing the way I buried the peculiar memories of my early childhood. It's the only way to preserve the false sense of normality that my life revolves around. *Just try to forget.*

My eyes snap open as I realize I've dozed off, perhaps for quite some time. The alarm clock reads 2 p.m. I sink my face back into my pillow, pulling the quilt tight over my shoulders. A gentle breeze sways the trees outside of my small stained-glass window, tossing the autumn leaves like a warm colored sea. I always found the fall comforting - not quite as bitterly cold as winter, yet not blazing with the heat of summer – a perfect balance.

Dragging myself out of bed, I throw on my gray hoodie, jeans, and slip into my worn tennis shoes. Glancing out the window, I notice the Dunkles' rickety blue truck is gone from the driveway. I'm surprised they decided to leave me alone in the house.

Descending from the attic, I make my way down the flight of stairs and into the kitchen. I grab a pack of crackers from the pantry, sure that they won't be missed by the greedy people in this house. Although I'm tempted to return to the refrigerator and snatch the steak once more, I resist the urge, stepping out of the kitchen and through the front door.

The sun's warm glow embraces me the moment I step outside. I breathe in deeply, absorbing in the clean green smell from all around. The Dunkles' house sits in the middle of nowhere, the nearest neighbor being well down the worn road. Encircling the house are tightly clustered trees, stretching across a few acres and adding a sense of vitality into the otherwise gloomy surroundings.

jumping down the porch steps, I stride across the grass and into the nearby bunch of trees, pulling myself up into one of their limbs. I climb higher until I grow nervous about the thin branches. Sitting on one close to the trunk of the tree, I place half of a cracker in my mouth. In the leaves nearby, a red robin flutters to an incomplete nest, carefully arranging a twig into the tangled branches before swiftly taking flight again. In a way, I envy the simple sense of purpose that guides its life. A drive to construct and provide for its future family. An aspiration that honestly proves to be a challenge for many humans. It's interesting how we view animals as primitive and simple, yet fail to replicate their seamless organization that comes solely from instinct.

    I feel connected to everything when I'm up here, clear-minded. Another escape that tends to make situations more bearable. I close my eyes and listen to the symphony of sounds carried by the wind, an array of bird chirps and squirrel scurries that I imagine into my happy birthday song. Unfortunately, joining their sounds is the roar of an old engine coming down the path.

Looking a ways downward, I can see the Dunkles' blue truck heading towards the house while trailing a cloud of dust. Quickly but carefully, I descend the branches and jump to the ground, running as fast as I can to the back door of the house. Just as I hear car doors closing, I scale the two flights of stairs to the attic.

Soon after, the house is filled with the Dunkles' obnoxious voices and laughter. Once again, I crash onto the bed after kicking off my shoes, slipping out my notepad that lies underneath the head of the mattress. Switching on the small lamp on the floor, I untie the thin string that binds the book together. On the pages are either journal entries or pencil drawings, depending on whatever mood had taken me that day.

Yesterday, I had drawn a detailed forest near a towering cliff, the silhouette of a woman standing near the edge under a fading mood. Usually, I draw whatever image comes to my
head, not realizing what my hand is creating until the entire picture is finished. I remove the stub of a drawing pencil from between the pages and begin sketching a curved line. As my hand glides across the paper, my

mind involuntarily flashes back to the mesmerizing light in the cellar.

    I hadn't imagined it, at least I desperately hope I didn't. No amount of imagination could have made it so vivid. But if it had actually been there, I can't shake this feeling of being more scared than anything, even more than second-guessing my own sanity. Maybe I inhaled too many fumes from that old gasoline lying around the cellar, or perhaps Harold tugged a few screws loose. Both explanations sound unlikely as they cross my mind, but they're all I've got to cling to.

*

    The sun has nearly set by the time my hand makes its final pencil stroke. On the paper is a detailed sketch of a long-haired girl, standing closely to a marble statue of a large horse. Her face wears a worried expression as she stares blankly from the page and into my own eyes, surrounded by an array of other statues and paintings against the wall behind her.

    Oddly, I find myself recognizing the scene—it's the one in the Pottstown Museum from the busier part of town that I've seen on television, even though I've never actually been there in person. There's an odd feeling in the pit of my stomach as I look into her shaded face, one of familiarity, almost.

    I close my notebook slowly, wrapping the thin string back around it. Just as I slide the book under the head of my bed, I hear the loud throaty voice of Mr. Dunkle yelling my name from downstairs. I let out a loud groan, aware that he only calls my name like that when he's furious about something I've supposedly done. I make my way down from the attic to the second-floor hallway. From the sounds coming from below, it seems like Harold is angrily ranting to Claretta about something I can't quite grasp.

    All three of the family's eyes burn in my direction as I walk timidly into the room. From the corner of my eye, I catch a mischievous expression on Declan's face as he slouches in the armchair at the back of the room. Claretta, arms crossed and legs folded, stiffly sits on the worn couch, while her husband leans on its back, his cheeks flushed in anger.

    "Where is it boy?" He growls, teeth clenched firmly together.

My eyes shift nervously from his face to Claretta's.

"W-what are you looking for exactly?" I stutter, hands sweating.

Harold lunges forward, grabbing me by the collar of my sweatshirt. "Don't play games with me, punk. I mean it."

"Please, honestly," I gasp out, "I have no idea what you're talking about!"
From the corner of the room, Declan's yellow teeth curl into a crooked grin.

"Why don't you check his book-bag, Dad? I think I may have seen him slip something in there yesterday."

I honestly wish the look I shoot at him would kill. Unfortunately, it doesn't, so my eyes look back up to Harold to anticipate his next move. His glare moves to my backpack that's sitting beside the front door. He releases me only to move swiftly to the bag, unzipping the front pouch quickly.

He removes the item wedged in between my schoolbooks, a tall bottle of his prized bourbon, kept only in a cabinet no one was to touch. My heart stops, knowing that I would never taken something of his, let alone something so sacred to him.

The outrage on Harold's face somehow becomes even more explosive. Anger boils in my own chest towards Declan, realizing he planted the bottle on me for revenge from last night. Before I can even turn to glare at him, the room violently shifts from under me as Mr. Dunkle's large, rough hand collides against my face with vision-shattering force.

I'm on the ground, stars scattering in front of my eyes. I can just make out something long and cylindrical in his hand as he pounds towards me, the wooden rod he keeps in the umbrella holder near the front door.
The thick wood crashes into my shoulder, then my ribcage, stealing the air from my lungs. Each blow forces a lump into my throat—not tears, but a colossal anger I'm desperately holding back. Both Claretta and Declan sit in their places, unmoved as Harold savagely

throws his swings. It is the final agonizing blow to my collar bone that triggers the unthinkable.

Just as he pulls back his arm for another swing, an intense burst of striking blue light suddenly tears through the air. A powerful, vibrating energy pulses through my body, enveloping me in heated waves that dance across my skin like electric currents.

Only a moment later, the sound of shattering glass and primal screams fill the room. As the tangible blue light fades, I see Harold lying amidst the shattered glass of a coffee table, clasping onto his right hand that holds the rod. As my vision steadies, I now see the reason for his agonizing pain. The exposed skin from his hand to the right side of his chest is now a charred layer of flesh, the wooden rod seemingly fused to the melted surface of his palm.

Claretta's high-pitched wailing pierces my ears, springing to the side of her writhing husband. She orders a bewildered Declan to call the police, attempting to peel Harold's shirt from the melted flesh to assess further damage.

The ground beneath me continues to toss uncontrollably. Adrenaline courses through me, completely numbing any injuries as I struggle to gather my thoughts. Mr. Dunkle's arm wasn't the only thing damaged in the flash, as charred streaks extend outward from me on the carpet and nearby walls.

In the kitchen, Declan verbally panics while on the phone with the police. He frantically explains how a foster kid, managed to burn his father's skin off in some inexplicable way.

I can't stay here, there's no way I can explain what happened to the authorities without winding up in prison or a psych ward.

I have to leave.

I sprint from the family room and upstairs to the attic as fast as my sore body will allow. Pulling on my sneakers, I speedily grab up whatever items I can think of, my notebook, a flashlight, a small Swiss army knife, and my quilt. With the items clutched in my arms, I abandon the attic without a second look, skipping steps in my rush to the front door. Dumping the objects in my book-bag, I look back at the Dunkle's in the room,

Harold clinging to his singed arm while a teary-eyed Claretta tends to him with a wet towel. She shoots a look full of hate and fear at me as I swing open the door.

Declan stands in the hallway a short distance from me with the phone in hand, a look of terror plastered on his face as our eyes meet. Under different circumstances, I would have reveled in my ability to strike this much fear into him.

I turn my back and step into the night, closing the door behind me. The moon is just setting itself in the sky as the sun sinks over the horizon, painting the world in a blanket of warm pink and orange streaks. With one deep breath in, I jump from the porch steps, and begin to run. I run the fastest that my legs will carry me through the thick trees, dodging their branches that become obscured under the moonlight.

Pumping through my veins is a rush of excitement accompanying undeniable fear. Something unexplainable is giving me the chance to escape from the prison that's surrounded me my entire life. The uncertainty now is if I have the strength inside to reach out and grasp the opportunity.

Chapter Three

*F*ire pulses through my legs and lungs as I emerge from the last stretch of trees on the Dunkle's property, each breath drawing the sting of the cold night air into my chest. Physical exertion has never been my strong suit, somehow I neglected to remember that.

The long stretch of road before me is completely desolate, dark trees stretching along its edge for quite some distance. I have some idea of where I'm going, though the daunting length of the journey lies ahead. Fortunately, most places in Pottstown are fairly close together. Unfortunately, this might also be a problem, considering the police will be on my trail if they aren't already.

I begin walking south on the side of the road, fatigue starting to slow my pace. The thoughts and pain that were temporarily warded off by an adrenaline rush gradually begin to cave in around me. Each place where the wooden rod had struck throbs with every heartbeat, especially the left side of my ribcage. Worse still are the flashbacks of what's happened in the past half hour.

I now know that the light in the cellar was real; limbs cannot be severely scorched by imagination. But is that a cause for relief? Knowing that I'm even more of a freak than was thought before? My mind ventures into any possible explanations I've gathered from comic books, ranging from alien abduction to radiation exposure. Again, clinging to any explanation that could perhaps make the reality of my situation clearer.

The minutes passing by as I tread down the side of the road feel more like hours, my fatigued legs growing heavier every second. The wind presses relentlessly against my back, tearing through my thin hoodie as if it were nothing. The few miles it will take for me to get to my destination seem like an eternity away, but I don't have any options but to move on.

From a distance, I can see faint flashes of red and blue, the sound of sirens reaching my ears soon after. A police car with an ambulance close behind it. I dart into the darkness of the leaves near me, ducking behind a thick bush. After a moment, both vehicles pass by me speedily, stirring up a trail of dust.

I pull myself off the ground, brushing the soil from my jeans. Far ahead down the road I can see that it branches out into three different directions, meaning I'm nearer where I plan to go. Yet, exhaustingly far away.

About half a mile past the break in the dirt road, I come to a dead end where the forest intersects the pavement. I hesitate before walking into the ominous trees, unable to help but feel a wave of chills as I peer into the darkness. After removing the flashlight from my bag, I flick it on and take a deep breath, stepping into the tangle of leaves and branches.

It only takes a few minutes of walking before I come to a break in the thick forest that opens into a small field. Near the center of it sits an old, abandoned barn house, overrun with weeds and surrounded by a decomposing wooden fence.

The overgrown vines and grass underfoot wrap around my ankles as my fatigued legs struggle to tear through them. Seeing the barn underneath the moonlight, my mind can't help but wander to childhood memories of playing inside it and in this empty field with the other children of the town. Several families ago, but it feels as if it were just yesterday.

The large doors had been boarded shut, but termite damage and time have made them brittle. With the little bit of strength I have left, I kick into the splintered wood until there is a large enough gap for me to squeeze through. The smell of mildew and dust clouds my nose the moment I step inside, the only light around coming from my flashlight as it cuts through the darkness.

Untamed grass and weeds sprout out from what's left of the floorboards underneath me, creeping up the sides of the walls as well. Moving my flashlight upwards, I see the loft above ground level that I remember dangerously playing on as a child, its supporting pillars seemingly untouched by the invading termites. Moving around the bales of hay on the ground, I approach the ladder that leads up to the loft, nearly tripping over a lamp that sits nearby. Unfortunately, it's an oil lamp that needs to be lit by a match, so I don't have a use for it. I move slowly up the rungs of the ladder, somewhat scared that one of them might snap under my weight. They remain sturdy, however, and I scan the area with my light as I make it to the top. The sight of rats scattering across the wooden surface forces a strained yell from my body. I remain frozen on the ladder; it takes a couple of minutes before I can pull myself off of it.

  With my flashlight searching around the dark corners, I carefully place my bag onto the floor and remove the quilt.

  I spread it across a small area of the dusty ground before I settle onto it. My skin tingles periodically, thinking of the small creatures creeping through the darkness around me. All I can do is pull my knees up to my chest with the flashlight in hand. Despite my discomfort, the sounds of the night soothe me in a way. The chirping of crickets, the call of an owl, the wind pressing gently against the walls of the barn. These sounds are the only things that would be able to coax me to sleep now.

I position my book-bag behind my head, looking up into the moonlight that breaks through a small crack in the ceiling. Despite the shelter of the four walls around me, the air is still undeniably cold, though not unbearable. I pull the sleeves of my sweatshirt over my hands, tucking into somewhat of a fetal position to draw in body heat.

With all of my strength, I attempt to force the restless thoughts of the past few days from my mind, but they come flooding in nevertheless. I don't have the slightest idea of where I'll be going; this farmhouse is not exactly the best option. Even if I were to attempt to run from this town, every pair of eyes will be looking out to report sightings of me sooner or later. News doesn't tend to travel very slowly around here.

Above every restless thought, the mysterious light towers over them all.

I keep believing this whole ordeal has been some kind of strange dream that I'll wake from soon. But with each passing minute, I'm becoming more aware that this is my new reality. My eyes close tightly, attempting to block out the darkness. Soon enough, my mind is thrown into the dream world, troubled thoughts close behind me.

*

I'm standing in the center of the busiest intersection in Pottstown, cars speeding around me without any hesitation. All stop lights seem to be ignored as floods of cars weave in between each other without breaking speed. Apart from the cars, the sidewalks and tightly knit buildings around me are abandoned; there isn't a person to be seen anywhere. Even the cars themselves show no faces through the tinted windows.

Directly in front of me through the intersection is a large pearly white building, decorative marble pillars stretching up along its sides. The words chiseled into the stone above it read "Pottstown Museum," gold trimming each of the letters. I step cautiously along the black pavement, just narrowly missing the cars whizzing by.

Soon enough, I find myself standing in front of the marble steps leading to the museum, with not a soul in sight through the large glass windows or in the doorway. As I push open the heavy glass doors, a cool draft rushes out to meet me. At first, my eyes see nothing, adjusting to the dim light. Gradually, the grain of the wooden floors and white walls trimmed in gold come into focus. The entranceway itself is plain, a line of metal detectors and a velvet rope cutting off this small section from the rest of the museum.

Stepping around the rope and detectors, I walk toward the tall arched opening that leads to the main areas of the building, my footsteps echoing against the walls. My eyes rise to the dizziness-inducing dome-shaped ceiling, tracing the lines of the colorfully painted birds and clouds that lie against its surface. Through the arch, I can immediately see the small paintings lining the walls. Strangely, as my eyes look into their frames, I see nothing but a blank canvas. This is the same for every painting as I walk down the long, wide hall.

Passing through another doorway, I see the empty paintings gradually fading into a walkway of statues. Animals and busts of stern-faced philosophers carved from stone stand frozen against the walls of the hall, their features so lifelike that a chill travels down my spine. From my peripheral vision, I swear that I can see their gazes trailing in my direction, but they return to their still forms as my head flips around.

Far at the end of the seemingly never-ending passageway, I can make out the form of a horse rearing up into the air. Its smooth marble surface glistens under a light source from overhead. As I come nearer to it, I can see a small, framed figure resting against the statue. A white-haired girl, her body so still I almost mistake her for another piece of art. The sudden movement of her beckoning hand assures me otherwise.

As her empty gray eyes meet mine, an unexplainable weight attaches itself to my legs, stopping me from walking forward. Even though I can't move, a mysterious force slowly pulls me closer to the porcelain-faced girl, the sound of her soft voice reaching out to me. Frighteningly, her words echo through my thoughts rather than in my ears, her lips never parting to speak

"Come quickly," says her wispy voice, *"We'll explain everything, don't be afraid."*

My mouth opens to speak, but no words can escape from my lips as an invisible hand presses against my throat. Sudden shadow falls against my back, stretching over the girl's now petrified expression.

Just as a pair of cold, clawed fingers wrap around my shoulders from behind, I feel my body being suddenly ripped from the ground, pulled into a wall of cold darkness that envelops the entire outside world.

CHAPTER FOUR

I jolt up from the hard ground, a sheen of cold sweat gathered on my neck and forehead. My heart pounds against my chest with each breath, even as it registers in my mind that it was merely a dream. Yet, it felt like more than that; I'm certain. Given everything happening around me, visions like this can't be taken lightly.

What strikes me suddenly is that this isn't the first time I've envisioned the girl in my dream; I'd sketched her in my notebook not long ago. Retrieving my bookbag from behind me, I unzip the opening and quickly take out my notepad. Flipping to the last-drawn page, I stare intently at the picture, my pulse still racing. Every detail sketched on the page mirrors precisely what I saw in my dream, down to the paintings on the wall and the girl's T-shirt and jeans. Somehow, deep in my heart, I sense that someone, or something, is attempting to communicate with me.

I can almost feel their presence. They're pulling me towards the museum across town. It feels like I have no other option but to go, even with the risk of being seen. "Everything will be explained," the girl's voice echoes in my head. Every bone in my body tells me that all the questions that have overflowed from my mind since my life started spiraling will be answered.

The realization that I'm clinging to hope derived from a mere dream makes me suddenly aware of my own desperation. But it's my last hope, and I have no choice but to embrace it. I gaze up into the crack in the ceiling, glimpsing the night sky. Judging from the fading moon, I suspect dawn isn't far away, and the air already carries the scent of morning. Pulling the quilt back up to my chin, I adjust myself on the uncomfortable floor. Once again, I must block out the images of rats scattered in the dark corners of the loft. Restless thoughts pry my eyes open until the light of dawn breaks through the cracks in the wooden walls.

*

I trudge through the thick trees again before the sun has fully risen, retracing my footsteps back to the main road. My pants legs and sneakers are almost soaked from the knee-high dew-covered grass slapping against my legs. The thin sweatshirt does little to protect me against the chilled morning air, so I pull its sleeves over my numbed hands.

Under daylight, the surrounding trees along the road are surprisingly pleasant, their warm colors tossing in the gentle breeze. My stomach suddenly growls violently, chewing into my back and reminding me of the length of time that's passed since I've had a decent meal. In my pocket, I only have a few dollars, enough for bus fare but not much else. The only thing to distract me from hunger are thoughts of what I'll find when I get to the museum. The fact that I'm driven only by superstition plants many doubts in my mind, but superstition is the most solid thing I have to hold on to at the moment.

It takes more than half an hour to walk to the closest bus station, right across the street from a small convenience store. It takes a good deal of strength not to go in to buy something small to eat. What doesn't help is the fact that the bus doesn't arrive for another good half hour, leaving me on the side of the road sitting on my book-bag until it pulls up to the faded bus sign, the fumes of gasoline clouding my nose. The white-haired bus driver says nothing as I step up, only eyeing me for a moment until I place my few dollars into the bucket near the front. The rows of seats are empty except for a heavy-set older gentleman in the back of the bus. I take a window seat close to the front, leaning my head against the glass. The bus's engine growls loudly as it pulls onto the road.

After minutes of looking out into the passing trees and small houses, I pull my notepad from inside my bag. Flipping to the picture of the girl once again, I study the images I had drawn, comparing them to my dream. Each vivid detail still lies fresh in my mind, from the imageless paintings to the empty world on the outside. My heart races suddenly as I remember the cold hands gripping me from the shadows, recalling the look of terror on the girl's face as she saw what was behind me. I close the book quickly, placing it back into my bag.

What catches my attention for a split second is a low playing radio that the driver just turned up slightly. Immediately, my heart rate quickens as I hear the words "foster child" and "Ethan Bennett" come from the newscaster's lips. My stomach churns as the speaker explains how this child attacked his foster parent, Harold Dunkle, in a brutal manner and may possibly face charges of arson and even attempted murder.

My ears shut off completely.

I feel dizzy, nauseous, a lump rises in my throat as I fight back vomit. With those few words, I'm realizing that my world is crumbling into a million pieces faster than I can comprehend. There's nothing to do but run.

Nothing I say could clear my name; what's an orphan child's word against a manipulative, conniving family.

I tenderly place my hand against my ribcage as the bruised flesh begins throbbing. Lifting my shirt, I can see the skin blackening where the rod had struck. The fear coursing through my body now joins with anger. Anger towards the Dunkles, and anger that their words would be taken for truth no matter what I say.

The bus ride lasts another twenty minutes before it comes to the stop near the busiest part of Pottstown. As I step off, I'm surrounded by lines of shops, stores, and tall apartment buildings, rushes of people going in and out of them hurriedly. I've never been at the center of town when it was this busy, perhaps because Halloween is days away, and it's a popular holiday in this town. All over, I see colorful decorations hanging from doorways and rooftops, the air almost warmed by the colors of autumn all around.

It suddenly occurs to me that if I was being spoken of on the radio, then I might have been displayed on TV. I pull the hood of my sweatshirt over my head, willing myself to become smaller as I hunch my shoulders. As I walk along the side of the line of brick buildings, none of the passing strangers show any sort of attention towards me, calming my racing pulse a little. The museum is close, I know, around the corner of this long stretch of buildings. As I walk past the windows of some of the shops, I can't help but stare at the baked goods through the glass, my mouth watering. Food will have to wait just a little while longer.

Around the corner from the last building, I can see a busy four-way intersection buzzing with a flow of cars. The similarity of all the details, from the traffic signs and stop lights to those in my dream, is uncanny. More shocking yet is when I see the gold-framed letters of the Pottstown Museum shining across the road. My pulse slowly begins rising as I come closer to the building, a busy intersection the only thing separating me from answers.

It takes forever before the pedestrian light declares it safe to cross, and I walk timidly across the white-lined pavement to the other side. Outside of the building is parked a school bus where a steady line of children flows out of it and onto the sidewalk. The museum's large wooden doors swing open constantly as townspeople dart in and out. Gripping my book-bag straps nervously, I walk up the concrete steps and to the heavy double doors. Before I can reach to open them, they swing open as a mother and her small daughter push through. I step through the open door, shoving my hands in my jacket pockets as the museum's powerful air conditioning rushes to meet me.

Immediately, there are several rows of people lined up behind metal detectors, a handful of security guards searching through any bags before they press through. My palms start sweating profusely, terrified that I'll be recognized. I can almost feel the cameras in the corners of the ceiling burning in my direction, and I pull my hood even further over my face.

The metal detectors are closer now, as is the burly guard dressed in a navy-blue uniform. Only a couple of people stand in between him and me, his jaw set tight as he searches through a woman's purse with unnecessary vigor. The beating in my chest triples as his glasses-framed eyes fall on me.

"Bag, please," he says monotonously. I remove it from my back and hand it to him quickly, making sure to keep my face down slightly. After rummaging through my bag for a moment, he allows me to walk through the metal detector. It remains silent as I walk under it, and the man hands me my bag.

"Have a nice day." he says almost grudgingly, his eyes lingering in my face a little too long for comfort. I can still feel his eyes fixed on me as I walk under the arched opening to the museum exhibits.

Unlike my dream, the frames that hang against the pearly white walls have beautiful paintings inside of them – colorful images of landscapes and detailed animals. Throughout the rooms of paintings are small groups of school children sitting cross-legged in front of the art as museum workers explain the history surrounding them.

Soon enough, I come to the hall of statues, each almost eerily lifelike in their detail. My head keeps turning behind me, positive I can feel their lifeless eyes trailing after me. From the corner of my eye, I can see two security guards looking in my direction from far down the hall, probing me before one of them speaks something into the walkie-talkie he's holding. I turn back around quickly, sighing deeply to control my panicked breathing.

Turning right around a corner, I come to the second passage of statues, slightly more dimly lit than the other. As I look down to the end of the hallway, my pulse quickens as I see a figure hidden underneath the shadow of the marble horse drawn in my notepad.

Half of the girl's face is hidden by the platinum blond hair streaming down to her shoulders, her arms folded tightly across her chest showing feelings of anxiety. She's wearing a light jean jacket with a white blouse underneath, the dark blue of her jeans almost matching mine. My body seems to move in slow motion as her light gray eyes meet mine.

    She looks deeply in my direction, almost studying me as I come closer to her. I look behind me once more, seeing that the security hasn't followed me around the corner just yet. I stand in front of the marble horse now, the girl leaning against its marble stand. She straightens herself as I slip off my hood.

    "You came." says her soft voice as she moves the hair from her face.

    Hearing a figment of my imagination speak puts me in a shocked silence for a moment.

    "But you already knew I would." I finally respond, tightening my trembling hands around my book bag straps. "Who are you?"

"A friend," Is all she responds with, unfolding her arms as she looks around nervously.

"I'll explain more to you, but we aren't safe here."

I look around at the few people observing the other statues on the wall.

"Who are you talking about?" My eyes lift to a security camera in the corner of the ceiling. "The security guards?"

"Something much worse, we have to leave now."

Her eyes widen as they look behind me. I flip my head around, seeing that the guards that had been scanning me before are turning around the corner with a couple other men in uniforms.

"Like I said," she whispers, gripping my arm, "Move now, talk later."

We break into a brisk jog down the passageway, exchanging quick glances as the guards pick up their pace, hot on our trail. It's evident now; they've pegged me. We navigate through the growing crowd, hoping the swarm of people would complicate their pursuit. My eyes dart around, scanning for possible exits. In the distance, I spot another hallway and she tugs my arm, guiding us left into the narrower corridor.

"C'mon, this way!"

The glowing exit sign at the end of the short passageway signals our escape, and we burst into a full run. The sudden flood of daylight pains my eyes, taking a few seconds to adjust. Now in a narrow alley between the museum and the adjacent building, the sounds of the busy street echo against the two brick walls. The girl gestures toward the back end of the alley, triggering a churn of suspicion in my stomach.

"Wait!" I call after her, "Before we go anywhere, you need to tell me what's going on. I don't even know your name."

"There'll be time for formalities in some time," says the sudden low voice of a man, "It's not safe for either of you here."

The stranger's voice startles me at first, unable to see who it belongs to. As I look around, I notice him leaning against the side of a large dumpster, hands tucked into the pockets of a brown leather jacket.

The seemingly middle-aged man's brawny build and intimidating stature catch me off guard. Most of the lower half of his face is hidden by a shortly trimmed beard, and gray-streaked brown hair contrasts against a pair of piercing blue eyes. The air of nobility that surrounds him adds to his intimidating presence, a strength I've never witnessed before.

Despite the initial surprise, I hurriedly, and perhaps stupidly, decide to follow both him and the white-haired girl around the corner of the alley.

The sound of the man's heavy boots bounces against the brick walls as we walk towards an unknown destination. Slowing to walk beside me, the girl breaks the silence.

"My name is Acia, by the way."

I nod, curious at the unique name. "I'm Ethan."

She grins subtly, "Yeah, I know."

My jaw tightens, "But how did you-"

"Your questions will be answered in due time," interrupts the man from ahead,

"But I'm afraid you might find yourself in some discomfort for a moment."

I turn to Acia with an almost panicked expression. "What is he talking abou-?"

Before I can finish, the massive man reaches back to grip both of our shoulders, pulling us after him towards the dead end of the alley. What happens next is nothing less than something drawn straight from my wildest dreams.

As we approach the end wall, a gust of strong wind blows into our faces, although there is no open area for it to flow from. Suddenly, the brick walls and the earth beneath us begin to shift and sway as if they're no longer made of solid material.

Instantly, they dissolve into a kaleidoscope of indescribable colors that surround us completely, any view of the outside world burning away with them like a flame to paper. I'm suspended in the air somehow, the ground underneath me no longer existent. Other than the sensation of the man's strong hand around my shoulder, I can't see, hear, or feel anything as the surrounding colors blend into an outer space like nothingness. The pounding of my own heart fills each of my senses as it pulses throughout my entire body, my lungs burning as the air becomes too thin to inhale. I attempt to scream, but no sound escapes from my lips.

A terrifying thought suddenly overcomes all others in my mind. *I'm dying.*

I can't think of any other way that it would feel like, my brain beginning to slow from lack of oxygen.

Just as I'm sure my consciousness is on the brink of fading out, another rush of air gently begins to blow through my face and hair. Slowly, the world begins to reconstruct itself from the inside out. The feelings in my limbs and body are the first to return, the sensation of pins and needles spreading through my skin and muscles.

A faint light reaches my eyes from some distance away, as if seeing it from the far end of a train tunnel. I'm aware now that I can feel earth under my feet once again, although it's quite softer from where I had been before.

As the details materialize in my surroundings, an irresistible force yanks me out of the darkness, as if breaking through an unseen barrier and thrusting me back into the tangible world. My legs give way, and I crumple to my knees, hands sinking into the sandy earth. *Sand?*

Before I can make sense of where I am, a feeling of nausea overwhelms me completely, forcing my stomach to heave up whatever is left in it.

"I apologize," comes a low voice from my right, "Traveling for the first time takes quite a toll on the body. I should've warned you."

I look up at the man, seeing only an outline of his shape with my swimming vision. "What the hell just happened?" I manage to choke out between heaving breaths.

"If you just follow us, you'll be able to understand."

The girl kneels beside me now, hand placed on my shoulder,

Taking another deep breath, I nod. My legs shake as I rise to my feet, pins and needles continuing to dance on my skin. As my eyes finally steady themselves, I can discern my surroundings in the dull light. Gradually, my brain recognizes the characteristics of a cave: countless large and small stalactites hang from the ceiling, light glistening against the moist surface of the walls. A wide path of white sand leads from where we stand to the cave exit. The sound of my heavy breaths echoes around us, and I attempt to quiet them.

Acia allows me to lean against her slightly as I walk on unsteady legs towards the light. Finally, as we come to the cave opening, the fresh smell of water blows against my face in a gentle breeze, the sound of crashing waves reaching my ears soon after. Once again, my breath stops completely as we step out into the open air. Never have I seen a view so beautiful, at least not outside of my dreams. Stretching out over the horizon is a glistening blue sea, waves crashing gently onto the pearly white sand of the beach. To my left stretches a low-standing cliff, the peaks of trees and greenery visible at the top of it. The cave we've just stepped out of is a gaping hole cut through the curved side of the cliff formation, its swirly white stone gleaming under the sunlight.

My legs slowly carry me to the damp stretch of sand, water from the waves gently lapping at my sneakers. I bend down and take up a handful of the stuff, letting it run back out through my fingers. I've never been close to the ocean before. This is more beautiful than I ever imagined it would be from watching it on the TV screen, and the sun kissing my skin almost makes me forget the bizarre way in which I arrived here.

I stand slowly, looking back at Acia and the man at the cave mouth as I brush off my pants.

"Are either one of you going to try to explain what's going on?"

Both look at each other for a moment, remaining silent.

"Listen," I almost shout, "Unless one of you starts talking, I'm not going anywhere else."

I realize how laughable my last statement sounds, considering I don't have much choice but to follow them.

Despite this, the solemn-faced man speaks.

"It's understandable that you have many questions, but if you want clear answers then you must follow us a little further."

I fold my arms around my chest, eyes rising over the cliff behind them.

"And where is it that we're going?"

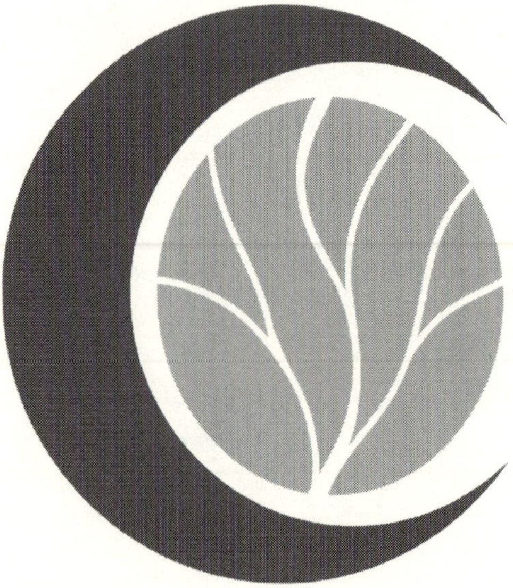

CHAPTER FIVE

On the far side of the white stone cliff, Acia and the still unnamed man lead me through a steep path of thick trees and vines on the side of the rock formation. I couldn't help but notice as we walked up the narrow pathway that it is strangely silent everywhere, not the slightest chirp of a bird or sign of insects. Except for the leaves swaying in the wind, everything is strangely still. Despite the breeze, beads of sweat form on my brow as we head further up. Quite abruptly, the man breaks the steady silence,

"Not much further to go, it's right over the bend ahead." although he fails to explain exactly what "it" is. The land curves gracefully, adorned with majestic oak and evergreen trees that stretch as far as the eye can see.

A tranquil lake, its surface shimmering under the gentle sunlight, immediately captures my attention.
Nestled a short distance beyond the lake is a charming wooden house. Despite its age, the reddish hue of the weathered wood exudes a comforting warmth, complemented by the ivy gracefully climbing its walls. The whole scene bathed in the soft glow of the setting sun nearly takes my breath away. On the crooked porch of the house, I can see the figure of a woman, her long silver hair fluttering in the passing wind. Her arms fold across her chest as she stands in wait, as if she's been expecting us.

    Once more, my heart sinks into my stomach as we approach her, the unknowns of everything around me creating a crushing pressure on my chest. What somewhat calms me is the smell of the air around this place—a mixture of lake water and honeysuckle bushes in the nearby trees. The woman carefully treads down the steps of the porch and towards us as we approach, a laced thin white robe trailing behind her. I can see that age has made her fragile, although there's an air of strength about her that doesn't coincide with her thin frame. A smile reaches up to her twinkling gray eyes as she steps down to meet me, surprisingly wrapping her arms around my shoulders in a tender embrace.

"You look so much like your father, my dear boy." she turns to the man standing a few steps behind me, tenderly placing a hand and my shoulder, "Does he not Horace?"

The man only nods slightly, looking down at his heavy boots.

Her wrinkled eyes turn back to me, "You have many questions I'm sure, my guess is that Horace wasn't very forthcoming on the journey?" her eyes flash disappointingly at him for a moment. I shake my head.

"Well then, you'll come with me, of course; we have much to speak about."

Her delicate hand reaches up to my cheek, eyes saddening. "You really do look so much like your father."

A lump rises in my throat hearing those words again. Never have I met anyone who spoke of either one of my parents with familiarity. It's that mere fact that persuades me to trust her, as weak of a reason as it may be. She takes my hand in her smaller one, pulling me towards the house. She looks back at the white-haired girl standing beside Horace.

"The others left to amuse themselves some time ago, you'll find them near the river." Acia nods, heading off to the trees on our left in a slight jog.

Others? My eyes follow her for a moment as she leaves us and through the thicket of tightly packed trees.

The woman leads me up the stairs of the creaking wooden porch, Horace staying behind.

Entering the house, I'm shocked that the inside seems much larger than the outside suggests. Vibrant colors and the crisp smell of pinewood floors rush in to greet me. The light blue walls of the entranceway are bare except for a couple of paintings of colorful wildflowers hanging on them.

The hallway, leading past a wooden staircase, takes me into a small kitchen with walls coated in light green wallpaper. Countless flowerpots and vines spread along the walls and windows, adding a breath of life to the space. I don't believe I've seen a kitchen so open and airy before; several door-length windows provide a view of the forest behind. A steady cool breeze carries the scent of nature throughout the house, helping to relieve my unsettled nerves.

The woman gestures to a wooden chair in front of a round glass table,

"Please, sit."

I do while she walks over to the stove to remove a steaming kettle, pouring a dark liquid into a teacup she pulled from the cabinet overhead. She places it in front of me as she sits in the chair beside mine.

"Tea to settle your mind," she says, "It's not the best but it's all I have here."

I nod, forcing a polite smile.

"Thank you, it's fine." I clear my throat softly, "Not to seem rude, but who are you? How did you know my father," I look out of the open window behind me, "-where is this place?"

The corners of her mouth curl into a slight smile,

"Of course, how rude of me,"

Taking a quick sip of tea, she continues.

"I'm Resmé, an old friend of your father's for quite some time before -"
She pauses, looking down at the cup in her hands.
"He was the best kind of man, your father. Honest as they come, loved your mother very much. She and you were his whole world."

I can feel a cold lump slowly rising in my throat. This is the most words I've ever heard spoken about my parents, especially regarding their relationship with me. All I feel is a longing to know more, yet dreading the truth of their demise. I couldn't stand to hear that right now. Seeming to sense my unease, the woman doesn't speak on them further.

"- But you will hear more of them in due time, you have other questions that must be answered." She stands, placing her pale green teacup on the glass table surface.
"Come with me, won't you."
I stand, following her to the open glass door a few yards from the table. She beckons me outside onto the small wooden patio that overlooks the edge of the hill that the

house is built on. The breeze ripples through my hair and clothes, carrying in scents from the ocean visible over the tree line. It suddenly strikes me that although it had been morning when I arrived at the museum a short time ago, the sun has already halfway set behind the horizon.

"Quite beautiful, isn't it?" Resmé sighs, interrupting my train of thought.

"Where exactly is this place?" I ask, leaning my chest against the thin wooden rail.

Resmé draws her lace robe in closer against the wind, looking up to the sky,
"To understand the answer to that question, you must open your mind to the prospect of something that you've learned to be impossible in your world."

My world? "What do you mean by that?" I ask, looking into her soft facial features.

"You're a smart young man Ethan, and perceptive. From the moment you stepped foot on the sand, you could feel the nature of this place surrounding you, could you not?"

My mouth opens to say of course not, but that would be a lie. I *could* feel something when I arrived. A knowledge in the bottom of my heart that I had been taken out of the world that surrounded me my whole life.

"We're not on Earth." I state, rather than ask. The realization somehow couldn't be clearer at this moment.

"You're not wrong," She responds, still looking over the horizon, "-although you're not entirely correct." Her eyes fall to a flowerpot near her feet, filled nearly to the brim with rainwater.

"Look into this pot for a moment." she says.

I do hesitantly.

"You're able to see your reflection?"

I nod slowly.

"Imagine this world as a small mirror image of your own, only with altered elements in the reflection. The planet remains the same more or less, but we're planted on a separate layer of it. I believe those in your world refer to it as-"

"A parallel world." I complete her sentence, the mere idea of it not registering as possible in my brain.

"In simple terms, yes. This is only one of the many other inner dimensional layers that can exist around us."

"How is that possible?" My eyes drift up to the warm colored sky, "How were we brought here?"

"I believe that may be more than you're able to comprehend in such a short period." She takes my hand gently in her own.
"But that will all become clearer at a later time. First, I would like to show you something, if you'll allow me to?"

I nod hesitantly, allowing her to cup my hand tighter in her own.

"Now you mustn't be frightened, just breathe freely."

I doubt that there's much that could scare me with this small- framed woman, but her statement does make me a bit uneasy, to say the least.

With her face only a short distance from my own, her soft gray eyes peer intently into mine, never blinking even once. That's when something strange begins to happen. The world surrounding us goes out of focus, her eyes appearing almost luminescent.

Within seconds, we are surrounded by complete blackness, her tight grip the only thing anchoring me to reality. The sound of my heart pounds through my ears, joined by my heavy breaths. Moments later, I can hear what sounds like gentle wind in the distance, tossing waves following soon after it. The world gradually begins to fade back in, first a light blue sky and the sun over the horizon.

Glistening water slowly reveals itself, the ocean smell reaching my nose. The ground beneath my feet is soft, the grass fading into a sandy beach several yards in front of us. The shadows of thick trees loom over our heads, sunlight just barely able to pierce through their leaves.

Under a beautiful oak tree some distance to our right is sitting a woman, a red blanket stretched under her as she holds a bundle of something close to her chest. As I look closer, I can see the bundle of tightly wound blankets is a sleeping baby.

"Who is she?" I ask Resmé, her hand still closed around mine.

"What is this place?"

She only tugs my hand after her, "Let us go closer."

We both walk softly across the grass; the woman doesn't look up as we approach.

"Excuse me miss?" I ask somewhat sheepishly. She's very beautiful I can see now, seemingly middle aged with not a strand of gray streaking through her curly brown hair. Her face appears tired as she looks down at the child, sunlight reflecting against her rich brown skin. Her hazel eyes are saddened almost to the point of tears.

"She can't hear you, or see you."
Resmé places her hand against the oak tree the woman sits under.

"She's not real. Neither is anything around us. It is all just the fabric of a memory."

"What do you mean? Whose memory?"

"We've stepped into the memories of your subconscious. You know where we are. You know who she is."

My eyes investigate the woman's face. The elegant curves of her cheeks and jawline, the glint in her eyes that I feel could light the darkness with a single smile. I do know who she is, perhaps not from memory, but from a pulling at my pounding heart. She's my mother. I'm the child wrapped in her arms.

All I can do is stare, mesmerized by this element of my life that's been buried for all these years. As my muscles go limp, my hand slips from Resmé's grasp. The moment I leave her touch, my mother, the ocean, and the world around me dissolves almost instantaneously.

I'm on my knees, once again placed on the deck of the lake house. Resmé's kneels to my eye level, placing a hand on my shoulder.

"W-why did you show me that?" I ask breathlessly, tears beginning to build in my eyes. Knowing the age I was when I was abandoned at the orphanage, this couldn't have been too long before.

"I want you to trust me Ethan," Resmé begins, "I want you to understand how much I'll be able to help you uncover. Unlocking your memories, and potential."

"What potential? There hasn't been anything special about me for my entire life."
The stark contrast of her words against my memories of years of struggling through the system is overwhelming. *Why care about me now? Where were you all my entire life?*

"I don't understand why you brought me here. I still have no idea who you people are, this is all just -"
Before I realize what I'm doing, I pull myself off the ground and sprint back through the kitchen door, passing through the house and out the front. I run across the grass until I reach the edge of the lake.

There's nowhere to go; I know that. No possibility of escape.

It's not that I feel like I'm in danger, but there's an undeniable feeling in my heart that if I stay, I'll have to come to terms with a part of my life that I never knew existed. *But is that something to be afraid of?*

Memories flash across my eyes of the many moments I've felt purposeless, powerless, and lost throughout my life. As I gaze at my reflection in the lake water, I come to the realization that I don't know who that person staring up at me is—apparently, I never have.

What I'm faced with now is an opportunity to uncover who that person is, and their purpose. But what

I'm already certain of is that the process will be terrifying.

"Running away already, are you?" Comes a bellowing voice from behind, Horace standing with his arms folded. "I had thought it might take longer."

"Quiet Horace, there's no need for your crudeness."Resmé approaches us, both having left the house after me.

"Ethan, could I please ask you to listen for a moment."
She catches my avoiding eyes. "I realize you must be incredibly troubled, but everything shall become clear in due time."

I look from her soft pleading face to Horace's scoffing one.

"'I imagine you have a great deal of questions concerning your abilities?" she says.

Immediately my mind goes to the powerful light that began this whole spiral into an unimaginable reality.

"How do you know about that?"

"Well, that's how we were able to finally locate you. The moment your powers were realized ,we were drawn to where you were."

"Why have you been looking for me? For how long?"

"We've been waiting for you to reveal yourself for many years, most of your life. Those are the questions we wish to answer for you, if you'll stay and listen."

I look long and hard into Resmé's eyes, looking deeply for any reason I should distrust her. But none of those feelings come. Somehow, I know her intentions are pure. I nod to her.

"Wonderful, walk with me, won't you?"

She leads me away from the lake and towards the line of trees stretching out around the house. The fading bits of sunlight cut through the spaces of the tree leaves above, creating various swaying shadows on the forest floor. Once again, there's not a single animal sound anywhere, not a flutter through the trees, not even an insect. The world is eerily still. Resmé breaks the silence.

"You're a special being Ethan. More unique than you could possibly imagine." she pauses for a moment, as though she's waiting for me to absorb the statement. "But with your unique destiny comes a world of threats."

A sudden chill runs down my spine.

"What do you mean by threats?"

"To understand that, you must first understand the history of our people. A story that takes place quite some time before your recorded history began."

She gently brushes her fingers through the low hanging leaves as we pass under them.

"Thousands of years ago, we were a great civilization that thrived on the untouched outer parts of our first world, Espareth.

The leaders of this place were gifted, advanced far beyond that of any other ancient civilization after them. This, in large part, was because of our ability to communicate with and manipulate the environment."

"Manipulate it? As in developing agriculture?"

Resmé sits herself on a nearby fallen tree stump, tearing a leaf from a small shrub near her.
"We called it the essence, a living power that flows through all that is around us. We were able to join into the nature of it, allowing us to connect to our environment as an extension of ourselves. It gave us a great amount of power."

Incredibly, the green leaf between her fingers begins to transform, morphing into the hues of autumn and dissolving into a mesmerizing swirl of golden dust. My eyes remain fixed in sheer amazement as the enchanted particles melt front between her fingertips and gracefully dissipate into the sky.

"So, magic - actually exists."
I sit on the soft grass in front of her, hands on my head.
"I'm honestly lost. It's just a bit overwhelming, processing all of this in a single day, you know?

Resmé laughs softly. "You've always known magic, some part of you has at least."

Could she be right?
I furrow my brows, the weight of her words sinking in. Absentmindedly, I pick a blade of grass from the ground, twirling it between my fingers as I gather my thoughts.

"You kept saying 'us'," I finally articulate, my voice wavering. "How were you one of them if you're saying this civilization existed *thousands* of years ago?"

"I once led a clan of my own, Guardians we were called. Each of us stood as the head of one of the eight Orders that made up our entire civilization. We allowed the essence to move through us as vessels, which preserved our life force for as long as it exists. All was well, each day was lived in peace and harmony. Until death and suffering entered our world as two of our sister clans initiated a rebellion."

"Everything sounds like it was working perfectly, what'd they find to fight over?"

"The clans and their Guardians were shadowed by greed. It wasn't enough that we shared the Essence as one body, they wished to possess complete power instead of portions. As their morals and good intent faded, so did the power running through their veins, as the Essence only flowed through those with pure intentions. So, they ostracized themselves from the other six clans, merging together and turning to darkness as another source."

Resmé rises from her position and continues to walk down the winding overgrown path, I follow close behind.

"They grew strong in dark magic as time passed, believing that the more strength they gained they would be able to forcefully bind the Essence to themselves. After their failure, they turned on the rest of our people - believing that in order to gain the remaining power, we must be destroyed.

Thousands of our people were killed, despite fighting with unwavering nobility. After one of the leaders of the rebelling Order was killed, only one remained to initiate the attacks against us. He came to be called Asdroth, a name our people gave to the malevolent. He grew powerful, feeding on the fear and evil that spread around us, until he nearly surpassed the abilities of us Guardians. It was then that we decided that the only way to preserve our people was to seal ourselves away from the destruction.

Merging all our power, we Guardians pierced a hole through the Earth's dimensional fabric, creating a pocket dimension of sorts; strong enough to shield ourselves from forces of death for years to come. Or so we thought. As the Asdroth core broke through, their magic quickly overwhelmed us and everything we built in the new world.

Fearing that all was lost, we six Guardians gathered together, bringing the strongest warriors from each of our Orders, six separate bloodlines. This gathering took place during the planetary eclipse that joins each of the infinite dimensions into an aligned strand for a single moment.

Using this event to aid our power, we drew in every fragment of Essence energy that our bodies could stand, directing the flow into the six warriors standing before us. The strain overwhelmed nearly all of the guardians, leaving only Horace and I alive."

"Horace - he's thousands of years old as well?"

"Yes, although his youth is preserved more than my own. The strain of maintaining access to this dimension has taken its toll on me over the centuries."

Resmé wrings her hands gently, seemingly distracted for a moment as she gazes at their thin, wrinkled skin.

"Our chosen warriors were endowed with multiple abilities once the eclipse resided;" she begins again, "- it was then that we began to be successful in our fight against the darkness. But the victories were short-lived as the sheer brutality of dark warriors nearly overwhelmed our forces, slaughtering half of the warriors mercilessly.

It was the sixth warrior who became our savior in the end. Unlike the others, Lycaneth's power seemed to have no limit; he held all their gifts combined, along with many more. The strongest power of Essence saw nobility in his heart, linking him directly to it.

Confronting Asdroth and his entire dark legion, he was able to defeat them by creating yet another pocket dimension that leads to the bowels of the universe. He sealed the opening with a seemingly unbreakable spell, ridding the world of the darkness forever. But this victory came with a price. The strain of such power overwhelmed him to the point of death, leaving behind an entire family to mourn him.

Our people then abandoned the new world we had founded, soiled by war and a great famine. Once we returned to the surface of the Earth, our people dispersed along the outside of the world, lacking leadership after the deaths of their guardians."

I hear the melodic flow of water nearby, a rushing stream emerging along the trail.

"I'm sorry for what your people went through; it truly sounds devastating, really. But, I don't see how any of this connects to me now."

"Patience, it will become quite clear to you in a moment. As our people merged with the rest of the world, it was realized that the essence had not left our blood. For each of the six warrior bloodlines, one child in their descendants was bestowed with the same gifts that had made their ancestors magnificent in battle. However, as the centuries passed, fewer and fewer of these emerged, mainly because their entire families had long since forgotten their otherworldly heritage, and the essence saw no need to manifest itself. That is, until the darkness began to emerge once again.

The spell Lycaneth used to entrap Asdroth's forces is bound by four ancient artifacts of our people. He stored his power within these ageless objects to act as anchors long after he passed. After these millennia, they're gradually being drained of the Essence bound to them. As they lose their power, the immortal darkness is able to unleash its evil little by little until it is able to break through completely.

"What I have to do with any of this. Just this morning I would've thought you were crazy if you said all of this existed. If there's something you think I'm supposed to do, I can't help you. I really can't."

Resmé sighs deeply, her face becoming hidden under the now rising moon.

"Ethan, the fate of this world has everything to do with you, who you were meant to be. I'm sure you've already recognized that you're unique, but you fail to realize just how crucial you-."

"- You keep saying that, but what dare you seeing in me that's so special? I've been alone for my entire life, where were you all? Why wasn't I so special to you back then?" I demand, my voice straining.

"Of course, you were just as meaningful to us. I've been searching for you and waiting until the emergence of your gifts from the moment I sensed your birth seventeen years ago. You're a child of the sixth bloodline, my son.
The very gifts that endowed Lycaneth with formidable strength against the darkness course through your veins.
Without you and your gifts on our side, Ethan, all will be lost."

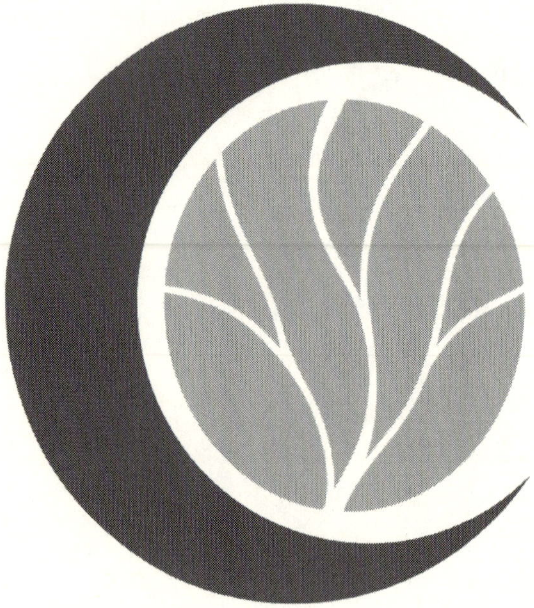

Chapter Six

Resmé's words echo through my head long after she says them. *'We need you Ethan'*... *'All will be lost'*. Never in my life has someone emphasized needing me for something, let alone considered me important. It's an odd feeling in the pit of my stomach, one of fear mostly, but also a sense of excitement.

This world offers me something I never believed I would have in a million years - a sense of purpose. However, overshadowing the excitement is the fact that everything I thought I knew about the world, myself, and my parents is about to change drastically.

Resmé and I begin to retrace our steps back in the direction of the lake house, the sun almost completely set.

"So how exactly did you find me after all this time?" I ask. "- and not to be rude, but why did it take so long? It was a little rough down there for a while."

She looks at me with a mixture of sorrow and understanding.

"I'm deeply sorry for the pain you endured for all of that time, the circumstances surrounding your emergence were not as straightforward as we would have hoped. There were complications, as your abilities didn't fully manifest until now."

She pauses, eyes lifting to the swirling sunset of purples & blues.

"The moment the first sign of your powers emerged I was able to sense it - many years ago when you were a boy, but they became dormant before I could fully locate you."

A sudden realization strikes me.

"The voices.' I utter quietly, "I wasn't going crazy, they were real – weren't they?"

"Entirely real. Your mind-sight was just beginning to surface before it was blocked off. My suspicions are that your subconscious veiled it for your own protection."

"Mind-sight?"

"One of the rarest gifts to possess. I was the only one to fully master it among the Guardians. It allows you to see into the minds of others, enter their dreams and memories."

"The girl, Acia. That's how she was able to get into my dreams?"

"Indeed, her connection to the first bloodline gives her abilities of the mind and spirit. She is one of my few remaining decedents."

"You said there are others, how many are here now?"

"Over the years I've brought in four, their parents murdered or missing from their childhood. The early emergence of their abilities made them a plain target for the remaining deformities of Asdroth roaming the Earth. Thankfully I was able to find them before they were killed."

"So that's why you brought us here, we're in a barrier of protection."

"Precisely. You all cannot be sensed by dark entities as your abilities grow here. The delayed discovery of your own abilities is what saved you from detection. With the merging of the five of you, Asdroth knows the prison dimension will be strengthened once again. He'll do all in his power to destroy you from afar, calling on his own corrupt bloodline."

There's a sudden pain in my stomach following the last part of her words. Shock is the only thing preventing me from completely breaking down mentally, as I realize the fears that haunted me throughout my childhood – the fears that I worked so hard to convince myself were a figment of my imagination - are revealing their reality. As real as the bruises pulsing underneath my sweatshirt.

We emerge from the dense trees, and the charming house comes into view bathed in the soft glow of moonlight. The comforting scent of burning wood wafts through the air, carried by a pillar of smoke rising from the stone chimney. On the front porch, four silhouettes are seated on the steps, leaning against the wooden pillars. Among them, Acia's distinctive white hair stands out as we approach.

"Well, I'll leave you to become acquainted while I finish supper." Resmé says, cutting in between the children and heading into the house.

My eyes lock with all four kids, close to my own age, I believe. No one speaks for one awkward moment, as if sizing me up. A tall, pale dark-haired boy beside the door speaks first, leaning against the wall with his arms folded.

"So, you're him huh?" he snickers subtly, "I thought you'd be just a little bit taller."

"Shut up Seth." says Acia, jabbing her elbow into his arm, "Don't mind him, he's still learning the ways of not being a jackass."
"- Doesn't seem to be learning very quickly though." Laughs a girl sitting on the steps, two raven-black braids falling over her rich brown shoulders down to her waist. "I'm Felicia."

I take her outstretched hand, feeling the delicate bones underneath her soft skin.

"I'm Ethan," I say awkwardly, caught off guard by the sharply curved features of her beautiful face.

"Yeah, we know who you are, dude," says the other boy sitting on the steps. He looks young, maybe about sixteen, with curly black hair contrasting against his olive-toned skin. He rises to fist bump my hand. "Resmé wouldn't shut up about ya since we got here. I'm Quinn."
"Well, it's nice to meet you guys."

I notice their hair is damp, as if they just finished swimming. Then I remember Resmé mentioning that they had gone to a water hole. I can't help but feel uncomfortable as I notice Seth's glare still burning in my direction.

"So, what's your thing?" Quinn asks, leaning against a pillar of the house.

"What do you mean?"

"You know, your powers. The reason we're all here. What can you do?"

Once again, I can feel all their eyes on me as they wait for me to speak. I grip my lower arm nervously.

"Uhm, I don't know yet exactly."

"Hmm, figures." Seth snickers, turning to go inside the house.

Acia rolls her eyes.

"Like I said, don't mind him. He's severely deprived of social skills."

"It's fine," I laugh shyly. "Nothing that I'm not used to."

"I've been here for years, and I'm still not used to it." says Quinn, "But let's go inside, smells like dinner's almost ready."

Just as the words leave his mouth, I'm aware of the painful clawing in my stomach. With all the happenings around me I forgot I haven't had a decent meal in almost two days.

The dining room exudes a modest charm, with floral decorations complementing the overall theme of the house. A long oak table dominates the space, adorned with carefully arranged plates and dishes of steaming, delicious food. A colorful assortment of vegetables, various breads, and a perfectly baked chicken.

I eagerly devour the food on my plate, my hunger taking over any semblance of table manners. A wave of embarrassment creeps down my spine once I hear a giggle from across the table. "I'm guessing they don't have food where you're from." Seth says with a grin, bringing a cup to his mouth. One stern look from Resmé across the table and the smirk disappears from his face.

"Where are you from anyway man?" Quinn asks.

"I was born in New Jersey, I think. Raised in Pennsylvania." I respond, noticing Quinn's mouth, which is so full it almost makes him look like a chipmunk.

"What about all of you?"

"Born and raised in Miami until I was twelve," Quinn responds first, "Resmé found me when I was on the streets and brought me here, almost five years ago."

"I lived in Far North Alaska with my mother until she—" Felicia pauses, face tightening as she pushes around the food on her plate. "—She died protecting me. I'm not sure how I escaped, but if it weren't for Resmé, I would've froze to death out there."

My eyes fall into my nearly empty plate. "I'm sorry about your parents. I know what that's like to go through."

"No point in being sorry." Seth scoffs. "I guess they didn't tell you that being part of this big happy family gets you a one-way ticket to orphan town. We're born to be hunted."

"Seth, that's enough." Resmé demands quietly yet sharply, her face set in a stern expression.

"But it's the truth," Seth says, folding his arms. "There's no point in sugar coating it."

"Nevertheless, I believe we've enjoyed your charm enough for one night," Resmé sighs, "You may leave the table."

Seth rolls his eyes before sliding his chair away from the dinner table and retreating upstairs.

"The boy is right, Resıné, although rash." Horace says, the power of his voice bouncing off the walls despite its low tone.

Resmé's eyes fall into the cup between her hands, before lifting up to meet mine.

"It is no matter of chance that you were all left orphaned. As I told you before, children who received the gifts of the bloodlines are hunted once their powers surface."

A lump rises in my throat, I'm unable to stuff it down.

"All of your parents who knew of their heritage did their best to prepare and remain hidden." Says Horace. " But there was only so much they could do to defend themselves once they were found."

"I brought in what killed them." My fist clenches underneath the table, and the lump in my throat grows even larger.

"Ethan no, you cannot blame-"

"-but it is my fault." I interrupt, standing up from my chair. I feel unstable suddenly, my heart steadily pumping faster inside of my chest. *They died because of you. You killed them.*

Before I realize it, I'm rushing from the house and into the night air. The same words keep echoing through my head as if someone is whispering them into my ear. *You killed them, you murdered your parents.*

I can feel the tears beginning well up inside my eyes, but I hold them in tightly. I haven't cried in a lifetime it seems.

The familiar feeling of weakness inside of me is nauseating. I vowed to myself that I would never let that feeling overcome me like it had in the past, and I stayed true to that vow the best I could for all of these years. But this…these thoughts are enough to break down every barricade that I thought I had built for myself.

I'm standing on the edge of the lake once again, staring down into the eyes of the boy looking back at me. A single tear breaks the reflection into ripples, thankfully obscuring my own face so I can't see the other tears falling. "*You're weak*" I spit at the reflection, wiping at my nose with the sleeve of my hoodie. "There's no point in blaming yourself." Horace's voice cuts through the darkness. I wipe my eyes quickly with both hands before turning to him behind me.

"They knew the destiny of their bloodline and sacrificed their lives to protect you, so that you may fulfill your purpose. Take their sacrifice and seize your destiny, so that it was not in vain."

"But I can't do this Horace, and I know you agree with me."

"Perhaps not now, you're a child. Untrained, irrational."

"Well, thanks for that." I turn back out to the lake, slightly offended.

Horace places a strong hand on my shoulder, "But we will train you. You *will* become the warrior you are meant to be, given time."

Somehow these words are reassuring, although hearing 'warrior' attached to my name makes my heart jump a bit.
"How much time do I have? From what I understand, there isn't much left."

"Very little time, within a month. Resmé will begin the first part of your training at dawn. But there's no guessing how long the remainder of your battle training will take."

My eyebrows raise. "I've never been a great fighter, I can tell you that now. What exactly is involved in battle training?"

Horace pats my back firmly.
"Get some rest. I imagine it's been an exhausting day for you."

I sigh deeply, "I honestly don't think you have any idea."

*

I stare blankly up at the ceiling of the small bedroom Resmé showed me. The sensation of a soft mattress beneath me is entirely unfamiliar, compared to the stiff, worn ones I had slept on for years. Unfortunately, my mind is so overloaded with thoughts that the prospect of sleep seems impossible. The absolute silence all around isn't helping much either; the only sound is the echo of my own anxious voice in my head.

In the span of twenty-four hours, every aspect of my life has been thrown into a dark unknown. What little I thought I knew about my parents and myself is shattered completely, and I don't know if I have the ability to fit the pieces back together. What's scarier to think about is the reality that I have no choice but to put my trust in complete strangers to help me find an entirely new life—one that, until yesterday, I wouldn't have believed to be possible.

CHAPTER SEVEN

With the morning sun comes a new air of hope in my heart. It's probably temporary; sunlight has a way of pushing all the dark thoughts from my mind for a short while. That doesn't stop me from wanting to hold onto the feeling for as long as possible.

Horace woke me up at the crack of dawn, the other children still asleep in the house. After giving me a hand-me-down pair of black cargo pants and a jacket, he guided me across the lakeside and through the line of trees to a nearby overhanging cliff, mentioning that Resmé would meet with me soon.

I don't know what waits for me now as I stare off alone into the distant horizon. I watch as warm rays of sunlight spread across the dull blue sky, reflecting against the tossing waves of water. I close my eyes, completely absorbing myself in everything around me—the light against my skin, ocean-tinted air rushing through my clothes, the gentle rumbling of the earth beneath me as the waves assault the base of the cliff.

"Beautiful, isn't it?"

I turn to Resmé as she approaches from the trees behind, her loosely fit blue gown fluttering gently in the wind.

"Very, I've never seen anything like this place."

She nods, smiling. "This small world has never been touched by man, stripped or polluted. Completely hidden."

I stand up from my place on the grass, brushing the dirt off the back of my pants, "Yeah, we do kind of have a way of screwing things up."

"Well, our people eventually drained our world of its very life force. Although reckless, your people have not reached that fate."

"Yet, anyway." I look back out to the water, "What have we come here for?"

"To begin the first phase of your preparation. I want to show you how to use one of the most powerful assets you possess. Your mind." She glides across the grass to stand beside me.

"The emblems I had spoken about to you yesterday, you're connected to them. Subconsciously linked to their magic."

"So, you want to get in my head like before? I'm not too sure how I feel about you going through stuff in there again."

"Not entirely, I'm not capable of uncovering hidden connections in your subconscious. Only you can do that, and I'm going to guide you through it."

I take a deep breath, "Then show me, please." Resmé nods gently, taking my hands in hers.

"Firstly, I want you to close your eyes, breathe. Focus on the feeling of everything around you. The breeze, the earth beneath your feet, the sound of the waves. Let it soak into your body."

With my eyes closed, I follow Resmé's instructions. I feel the wind against my skin, absorb the sunlight into myself, and connect with all the sensations and sounds as if they were an extension of my body.

"Now," Resmé whispers gently, "close it all out slowly. Draw your focus to a memory from your past, the earliest one you're able to reach, even if it's just a feeling. Picture your surroundings from that moment, make them real."

Just as she tells me, I slowly begin to close out the sensations from around me one by one, channeling my focus into sorting through my memories.

I find one, a dark image in my mind that's so distant that I'm not even sure if it's an actual memory. More like the shadow of a memory, one that's been fading over the years of my lifetime. Slowly, I pull the details into reality, carefully painting each one in the darkness of my closed eyelids.

All at once, I feel the world stop. The wind against my skin disappears, as does the sound of the waves. I can no longer feel the sunlight on my face or smell the scent of the trees. The only sensations remaining are Resmé's hands in mine, and the cold, hard earth. I open my eyes to complete darkness, unable to see my own hand in front of me.

"What is this?" I ask, my voice echoing throughout the thick blackness as if it were a cave. I take a step forward, feeling the harsh rock surface beneath my feet. *"This can't be my memory; I don't know where we are."* I think to myself; although to my surprise, my voice projects from my mind into the air as if I had spoken. I begin to walk at a slow pace, hands outstretched in front of me.

Just as I am beginning to believe there is nothing but empty space, I'm suddenly aware that Resmé is no longer beside me. I turn around frantically, calling out her name. Complete silence. My heartbeat rises into my ears, and my walking pace turns into a run. I don't know what I'm running to or away from, but the overwhelming feeling of the unknown is more than I can bear.

    I stumble over something in my path and fall to the ground, scraping the palm of my hand. I feel for the object that tripped me and find it beside my ankle. I believe it to be a large rock at first, but I soon feel that it is far too brittle. My fingers trace the outline of two large sunken holes, with a smaller one slightly beneath them. As my fingertips brush against the angular shape of a jaw, and rows of cracked teeth, I realize the horrific object I'm holding in my hand—a human skull.

    With a yell, I hurl the skull far away from me, frantically springing to my feet. I hear loud cracking beneath me, more
bones. Thousands of them, there must be. With every stride I take, the sound of snapping carcasses pierces my ears.

    I'm surrounded by death, the stench of it now flowing upward to grip my very insides. I finally collapse, landing on my hands and knees.

    As I kneel gasping, a soft echo reaches my ears from the darkness.

"Ethan" a voice calls out, *"Come to us Ethan, we've missed you."* The voice is not that of a man, or a woman. It carries layers, as if a chorus of wispy-toned spirits speaking in unison.

Somehow, I can sense a power in it, something ancient, something beyond any evil I have ever felt before. The voice repeats its eerie invitation, growing louder with each iteration.

A dim light in front of me catches my eye, radiating from the ground like a smoldering fire. As I approach slowly, I realize the light emanates from a deep hole only yards away—a wide-mouthed abyss that appears to have no end. The fiery light crawls up the walls of the chasm, growing brighter as it nears the surface.

I'm able to see my surroundings, at least those close to the hole's edge. My throat tightens with horror as I see the floor of skeletons surrounding the dark opening and under my own feet. Abruptly, the ground begins to shift and sway, throwing me to the ground as the tossing becomes violent.

I'm starting to hyperventilate as the sea of skeletons begins pulling towards the abyss like a tide into the sea, dragging me helplessly with it. With each desperate attempt to fight the flow of bones, I'm pushed hopelessly to my knees as the flow pours faster into the glowing mouth.

As I grow dangerously close to the chasm's edge, I can hear them. Thousands of blood-curdling screams escaping from the depths of the earth. My own screams join them as I frantically flail my arms to grab a hold of something, anything. There is nothing but bones, the stench of death growing stronger as my body hangs helplessly.

I yell in pain as a bony claw grips around my ankle, its touch searing like melted iron against my skin as it rips me from the edge.

Another strong hand suddenly grabs my wrist from above, pulling me from the creature's grip.

My eyes fly open wildly, mouth gasping for air as I emerge from the hellish nightmare. Resmé kneels over me, hands tightly pressed around my face.

"I'm so sorry," she cries, "I tried to pull you out from the beginning, something went terribly wrong."

"What the hell happened?" I cough, my lungs still burning. The air is colder than it was before, and there are no bright beams of sunlight breaking through the clouds.

"Your mind, it slipped from my grasp somehow. You pulled away from me."

"Pulled away to where? That wasn't my memory, I've never felt anything like that before in my entire life."

A sudden burning sensation sears my right ankle, and I hiss in pain, quickly pulling up my pant leg. My eyes widen in horror as I observe the bright red traces of long, narrow fingers burned into the skin of my ankle. Resmé's breath catches.

"This shouldn't be possible, not yet."

"What's happening? How could I be hurt if none of that was real."

"Harm done in your astral form may translate to your physical. The dark forces that wish to enter this world are able to sense your abilities. They're desperate, I didn't think you could be accessed this quickly, I am truly sorry."

I stare in disbelief at my reddened flesh, an overwhelming fear welling up inside of me.
Resmé helps me back to the house, wrapping my ankle in a cool damp cloth as I lay in my room.
She leaves me to rest, although my mind is racing much too quickly to even consider this. Frantically, I draw an image of the horrifying abyss in my journal, the details becoming more profound as I allow my mind to travel back into that darkness. I can hear the voice echoing through my own ears, like something eerily familiar—something from my deepest nightmare.
"Come to us, Ethan. We've missed you."

I look up from my page as there's a knock on the doorframe. Felicia stands with a concerned look on her face, dressed in an oversized plain white T shirt and pajama pants. I assume she's just gotten out of bed.

"Resmé told me what happened to your leg, do you mind if I take a look?" She strides over to my bed without waiting for an answer, lifting the damp cloth to expose my burn.

"Hey!" I flinch, moving to cover my ankle. It didn't hurt much, I just don't much like the idea of appearing weak and injured to a girl I just met - stupid, I know.

"It's okay," she insists, "I can help."

I hesitate, but allow her to gently cup my ankle in her hands. Somehow, her touch instantly cools the burning that has not let up for hours. She closes her eyes, and I watch in astonishment as a gentle golden glow spreads from under the skin of her forearms to her fingertips, growing brighter as it reaches the skin around my ankle. At first, there is an odd tingling sensation that spreads into my calf, almost like pins and needles. As the glow spreads through my skin, I can see the silhouettes of my veins and leg bones as if I were watching an x-ray. My eyes widen in amazement as I watch my burned skin slowly fade away, as if it were a stain washed by water. The glow fades, revealing my skin to be completely unmarked.

I stare down at my leg, awestruck.

Felicia laughs, patting my ankle. "I know it's a bit weird when you first start seeing this stuff. I'm a Fourth Blood, a healer, that's my thing."

"T-that's so amazing" I utter, "Like, unbelievable really. I feel like a 'thank you' isn't enough."

Feeling my chest and shoulder, I realize I'm no longer bruised from Mr. Dunkle's attack.

"Don't sweat it. Kind of a rough way to start your first day huh?" She takes a seat at the foot of my bed.

"What happened down there anyway? Resmé seemed pretty freaked talking to Horace about it."

My eyes fall to my journal closed in my lap. "She was trying to help me sort through memories, but something else made its way in." I open the pages to the picture I'd just drawn. "Something that wasn't one of my memories, it hurt me somehow."

Felicia's eyes trace over the images of skulls, and the wide mouth of the glowing abyss. A moment of fear flashes across her face.

"You're going to see a lot of things that don't make sense now, and most of them might scare you at first." She reaches over to close my journal before walking back to the door.

"But it's up to you to decide if you're going to allow those things to prevent you from figuring out your truth. Ignore whatever that thing is for now and get stronger with your training. You'll have time to worry later, trust me."

Chapter Eight

I slept well throughout the night, even as nightmarish images continued to flash behind my eyes. Felicia's healing touch seems to have energized me on top of healing my wound. Resmé suggests that I meet with Horace and the rest of my housemates to spectate as they train in an open valley nearby. Searching through the bag of clothing I was given by Resmé, I slip on a fitted white shirt, black jogger-style pants and sturdy calf-length boots that I assume belonged to one of the boys in the house.

I follow a pathway through the forest that Resmé directs me to until I reach the large green valley where my peers and Horace are training. Once I break through the thick stretch of trees, my breath catches as a large circular stone platform comes into view, four stone pillars standing on the outer edges.

I'm instantly reminded of the Stonehenge in our world, ancient and ruined, yet strong and beautiful.

Within the stone surface, weathered by time, various symbols and images have been intricately carved, nearly eroded but still holding a whisper of their history.

Quinn and Seth position themselves on opposite ends of the platform, securing their wrists with what appear to be cloth strips. Sunlight glints against the black pieces of armor protecting their neck, chest, and shoulders.

I walk over to Horace, who sits on a large rectangular stone at the circle's edge, his expression stern. Without a word, he raises his right hand into the air as Quinn and Seth both face one another. His hand drops quickly, and before my eyes can register, they're fighting against one another in an intense grappling and striking match.

Quinn's movements are a dance of precision, effortlessly dodging Seth's jabs and executing a swift leg sweep that sends him sprawling to the ground, defying his smaller stature. In a desperate attempt to break free, Seth retaliates with a vicious elbow strike, connecting with the bridge of Quinn's nose.

Ribbons of blood erupt instantly, staining the air with a visceral intensity. Concerned, I turn to Horace, but his expression remains stoic; a bit unsettling considering the chaos unfolding.

Is this not too far for a training session?

Quinn stumbles backwards while holding onto his nose, his face flush with anger.

Realizing the damage he's caused, Seth's smug expression shifts quickly once he sees Quinn's rage. Blood cascades from Quinn's nose, forming a dark pool on the stone ground, while an ethereal silvery-blue glow rises like steam from his skin.

In a sudden surge of unrestrained fury, Quinn launches himself toward Seth, and what unfolds next defies the limits of my brain's acceptance of reality.

Within an instant, Quinn's limbs and body undergo a startling transformation, elongating and contorting. His once-curly black hair fades into a platinum cascade across his skin. Razor sharp claws sprout from his fingertips, his face assuming the features of a massive feline.

Transformed into a snow-white panther, Quinn now stands twice the size of what I believe the creatures should be. Stumbling backward in sheer astonishment, I instinctively crouch behind Horace's stone for a semblance of protection, though my gaze remains fixed on the circle's center.

Seth's movements are swift, not necessarily superhumanly fast, but agile enough to evade Quinn's repeated pounces.

Vaulting into the air from one of the pillars, Seth deftly plucks a strand of fur from Quinn's back. The panther halts its attack, fixating on Seth's hand as he examines the fur between his fingers.

His gaze locks onto Quinn's, the whites around his pupils swiftly turning as black as ink. The panther's eyes mirror the transformation, and he stumbles within the stone circle as if he's suddenly blind.

What the hell is happening right now?' I scream in my head repeatedly, unable to comprehend the surreal scene unfolding before me, as if it were ripped from a wizarding movie.

"Seth creates illusions."

I turn around towards the voice, seeing Acia step through the tree line.

"He can make you feel anything, see anything, or see nothing if he wants."

I look back to the circle, seeing that Quinn's shifted back into his human form. He feels along the ground, sightless and naked as Seth claps his hands slowly.

"I promise that's the closest you'll ever get your dirty paws to me buddy boy. Pathetic really-"

"Seth!" Echoes Horace's voice finally, "That's enough, the exercise is over. Return his sight."

Seth stares Horace down for a moment, his fist clenched so tightly his knuckles turn white.
After taking a deep breath, the inky black melts away from his eyes.

Acia runs over to Quinn to throw her jacket over him.

"What the hell is wrong with you?" She growls at Seth,

"What did Resmé tell you about going to far, it's dangerous and awful!"

"Oh shut up, he came at me first I simply retaliated."

"You also drew first blood. We've talked about it; we don't train to hurt one another."

Acia helps Quinn cover himself as he walks slowly from the circle while holding his bloody nose.

"You've had quite enough for the day Seth." Horace stands from his place on the boulder, brushing the dust from his trench coat.

"No, I want to get the new kid up to speed first." Seth grins at me, arrogantly waving me towards him.

A lump forms in my throat, but I quickly swallow it down. If there's one thing I have experience in, it's taking care of bullies back at home.

"He's had no form of teaching, leave it be and go wash up." Horace commands.

"So, you're saying that he's a coward? Half of us have been fighting since before we got here." He smirks. "Pity."

My fist clenches as I step quickly towards the stone circle. "I'm not afraid of you, c'mon let's go."

Horace lifts his hand, "Ethan no, you must wait-"

I stop listening. Tunnel vision is overtaking me again, just like with Declan Dunkle, his father, and every other bully in my life. What I don't anticipate is how quickly the grip of his stare takes hold of me.

Seth is tall and strong, his raven-black hair and glaring eyes adding to his slightly intimidating presence. My legs carry me closer to him, and my fists instinctively rise before I can even realize. He smirks again.

"Go ahead, I'll even let you swing firs-"

My clenched fist launches towards him before he can finish. He dodges it swiftly, grabbing my wrist and sweeping his leg under mine, throwing me to the ground with his entire strength.

It hurts, a lot more than I anticipated. All the breath in my body is knocked out against the cold stone. I gasp for air, holding my chest tightly.

Seth stands over me, his stupid grin showing once again.

"Disappointing, really. You have a lot of work to do." He roughly tussles my hair, I feel a slight pinch as he yanks a hair from my head."

Grabbing his wrist as he did mine, I kick his legs from under him and he falls to the ground. I'm up again and backing away to gain my footing.

As Seth crouches on the ground, I see that his fingers still hold on to the hair from my head. He wraps it around both index finger, winding it tightly between them. As his eyes glare at my own, I can see them slowly becoming black as ink like before.

Suddenly, I hear his voice clearly in my ears, although his lips remain still.

"Let's find out what kind of things you're afraid of kid."

He's in my head.

Without any warning, complete darkness closes over my eyes. There isn't a single sound, or single beam of light.

Ah shit Ethan - I swear to myself, now regretting my decision to fight. *What have I gotten myself into?* All at once, I'm surrounded by a dense, dark forest. A bright half-moon beams above me, although it doesn't much lighten my surroundings. In front of me the ground seems to sink into a large dark hole, a dark red glow emanating from the very bottom of it. A snarky laugh echoes through my ears and all around me, reminding me that all that I'm seeing is only an illusion cast by Seth.

"Quit it, let me out!" I try to yell, but no sound escapes my lips. The earth beneath me begins to shift and slide towards the entrance of the abyss, dragging the surrounding trees with it. With all my strength I claw at the sliding dirt trying to make my way towards something solid, but it's no use.

The same fear that I had experienced in the vision with Resmé radiates through me again, my heart pounding through my chest until I feel like liquid fire is running through my veins. There's a pressure building in my body, a pressure that releases itself in a wave of heat that leaps off of my skin.

In the blink of an eye, the air and entire ground beneath me bursts into blinding blue flames. I can't see anything, only feeling the intense heat surrounding me. Despite being completely terrified, I realize that I'm not burning. I don't feel the ground shifting underneath me either. The only sensation I can feel is a static-like layer in the air, similar to brushing your hands against an old TV.

Once the light clears, I'm standing once again in the stone circle.

I'm horrified to see it ablaze with tall blue flames, long trails of fire rippling through the cracks and symbols in the stone. Seth lies on the ground several yards away from me, his face showing pure fear as he's surrounded by a circle of fire.

I can hear the muffled voices of Horace, Acia and Felicia seemingly shouting from the outside of the circle, but they're blocked off by the wall of flames. I'm unable to move, either frozen with fear or shock. With each pound of my heart, the flames around me pulse and spread outward, although never coming close to me. This is when I realize.

I'm creating the fire.

As my heart falls into my stomach, I unclench my tightly squeezed fists.

Just as suddenly as it had begun, the blue flames melt away into nothing, leaving behind swirling charred trails in the stone all around.

My heart still pounds in my ears, everything around me seems to be moving in slow motion. As my vision begins to blur, I can just barely make out Horace heading towards me and Felicia approaching Seth's side.

"I'm sorry, I didn't mean to-" Are the last words that I'm able to speak before the world spins under me, and I fall to the ground.

CHAPTER NINE

The room is completely dark when I open my eyes. The entire day must have passed since I collapsed. When I try to sit up, the muscles in my back are so sore and stiff I'm unable to move for a moment. Gritting my teeth, I swing my legs over the side of my bed and pull myself up painfully.

What the hell did I do to myself?

I'm extremely thirsty, So I begin walking slowly through my doorway and into the hallway. The wooden floorboards creak loudly with every step, reminding me of those journeys from my old attic in the Dunkles' house. From the top of the stairs, I can hear that someone is also awake despite the late hour.

Making my way to the kitchen, I see Resmé in yet another flowing white gown next to the stove, pouring hot tea into a cup. One steaming cup is already resting on the table.

"Won't you sit with me for a little while?" She beckons. I realize she'd already prepared a cup for me.

"I'm really sorry for earlier," I apologize before I sit. "I don't understand what happened, honestly. Seems to be a lot of that going on lately."

Resmé nods, gesturing towards the chair again as she takes a seat.

"This environment is fueling your abilities faster than you can learn to control your emotions. I hadn't expected it to begin this quickly."

I sit down with her.

"That fire, I could have hurt someone. I couldn't control it at all."

"But you calmed the flames, did you not? That shows me you possess restraint. The hardest element to teach."

I look down at the steam rising from my cup of floral smelling tea.

"What am I? I mean, what exactly am I supposed to be able to do? Everyone here seems to have a grasp on their abilities."

I bring my hand up to the light of the lamp hanging above.

"One minute I'm able to do one thing, the next minute it's something else. It's confusing, and a bit scary."

"The spontaneity of your abilities is what makes you a powerful force. As the Sixth Blood, you hold access to many different powers. You're young and learning, they may manifest in various...unstable ways."

"But for how long?" I look down at my hands, "I've hurt someone back at home before, not on purpose, but still, it wasn't the best time at all."

"The state of your emotions has the power to destroy, or to create. You need only to train the condition of your mind, restrain your power a bit."

Resmé gently lifts her right hand. Almost instantly, the wooden walls, floor, plants, table, and everything else in the kitchen melt away in a silvery wave of dust.

A cool breeze flows against my skin, the sound of brushing tree leaves whispering through the air. We're suddenly standing in the center of the stone training circle in the dim forest, dull beams of morning sunlight beginning to peek over the horizon.

"I'm never going to get used to that." I say, hunching over slightly from sudden nausea. Luckily, it fades quickly.

"You'll learn this ability yourself soon enough. Spatial tampering took us a millennium to fully master."

Resmé brushes her bare foot against the charr marks I had created in the stone earlier in the day.

"The Sixth Blood's gifts first manifest through the elements while their abilities are in rawest form. All emotion and instinct, no control."

She waves her hand slightly over the stone ground in front of her.

Within an instant, a circle of fire bursts around me faster than I can possibly react. The heat surrounds me without hesitation, singing my bare feet.

"What are you doing?!" I shout over the roar of the flames, bringing up my hands to shield my face.

Resmé's voice echoes through my ears. "You're in control, Ethan. Breathe, and simply speak to the essence of the flames. Calm them"

As the flames grow closer, an intense panic attempts to overcome me. Somehow, I hold it at bay with a slow steady breath.

Speak to the flames.

Raising the palm of hand toward the scorching heat, I direct the breath from my body outwards, imagining a cooling wave washing around me.

"*Calm.*" I whisper.

Instantly, the raging red flames shift into a silvery blue. The radiating heat suddenly becomes a refreshing cool breeze as the fire melts upwards into the night sky.

Resmé places her hand on my shoulder as the last of the shining particles fade away.

"All of our power lies within intent and feeling. You

must see the essence as an extension of yourself to reach your full potential."

I look down at my hands, the same ones that have carried me through all the struggles that life has dealt me up to this point. Suddenly, I don't recognize them as mine any longer. They're capable of more than I ever could have ever dreamed of before. Capable of magic, capable of saving the world.

"Horace said that I have a little less than a month to prepare, where are we going once I'm ready?"

Resmé leans against the stone pillars of the training circle.
"Once we're able to see the emblem locations through your subconscious, we'll be able to gather them."

"What about the people after me, what happens if I'm not able to get to the emblems first?"

"Children of the Asdroth core are not people, they're physical manifestations of suffering and darkness. Some of them acquire bodies of heartless humans, others remain in their natural form."

A chill runs across my skin. "What is their natural form? What are they?"

Resmé looks down at her clenched hands. "There's no need to fill your head with horrible images more than it already is. With our protection, you won't encounter them. But you *will* learn to fight."

Chapter Ten

Just as the sun has risen, I find myself standing within an open circle of ancient towering oak trees. Their branches twist and weave to create a dense natural enclosure in the center of the forest. Horace has guided me here for my morning training, very much against my will as I'm extremely tired and sore from yesterday. Still, I'm comforted by the crisp earthy undertones of the air while a distant stream trickles gently in the background.

"So, to begin" he says gently. "The true mastery of your abilities goes beyond control; it delves into the very essence of your powers. Feel the life force coursing through the trees, the air, the earth and yourself. They're all interconnected."

I breathe in deeply, once again attempting to attune my senses to the natural symphony around me— the whispers of the wind, the pulsating life within the forest.

"Today, I'll guide you in harnessing the essence of change within a living being," He continues, gesturing towards the tangle of green. "The trees before us, reach deep into their branches, and paint their leaves with the colors of autumn."

I turn towards the towering giants, their lush green leaves shimmering under the interplay of sunlight and shadow. I extended my hand toward them, slightly unsteady from anxious nerves. Horace's reassuring touch lands on my shoulder.

"Remember, your abilities flow through intent, emotion and vision. To alter the leaves, you must visualize and feel the change beforehand."

Closing my eyes, I focus on memories of autumn from back home —the brisk breeze, the sweet scent of fallen leaves, and the vibrant palette of warm colors; the fiery reds and sunlit yellow fields back at the Dunkles. In my mind's eye, I look intently into a single green leaf of the tree before me, drawing it closer until I'm able to see a clear image of the veins running throughout its surface.

My heartbeat quickens as I exhale, visualizing a wave of gold washing across the leaf like fire spreads along paper. I project the vision and extend my hand towards the waiting tree, attempting to hold on to the pleasant emotions from my memory.

Opening my eyes slowly, my breath catches as the vibrant green begins to melt away. Gradually, each leaf shifts into warm reds, oranges & browns as a light breeze waves through them. The beautiful colors spread from this one tree into another, and another. Soon enough, Horace and I are surrounded by a tossing sea of autumn colors. Even the air is now filled with a slightly sweet scent.

Horace smiles encouragingly, gently placing his hand on my shoulder. "I hope you're beginning to understand the intricate connection between your emotions and your abilities. After some time, you'll find that you hold the ability to shape the very fabric of the world around you. Until then, patience."

*

Horace and the others are once again training as the sun just reaches the horizon. Resme' directs me to their place on the beach where I first arrived.

From a distance I can see objects flashing in their hands, along with the clear sound of metal clashing together. Once I make it across the sandy slope over to them, I can see clearly that Acia and Quinn are sparring intensely with swords inside of a large drawn circle.

I'm immediately awestruck by how graceful, yet fierce Acia appears with the weapon, easily weaving around Quinn's swings before disarming him with a slight twist of her wrist. She moves with ease, as if performing an intricate dance.

Quinn laughs, his arms held up.

"I surrender madam, don't dice me up please."

Acia smiles, picking his sword and handing it to him.

"Your instincts are getting much better, keep it up." She turns over to me as I reach the edge of the circle.

"I was wondering where you were, glad you didn't run away."

I laugh a little, waving to the others sheepishly.

"Not yet anyway."

Seth scowls at me from the other side of the training circle. I don't pay him any mind, looking over to Horace.

"You mind if I give this a shot?"

He nods over to Acia. "Just take it easy on him. Don't want to scare him off too quickly."

Quinn hands me his sword as he walks out of the circle, patting me on the back.

"Good luck buddy, just remember to watch the hands, not the face."

The sword is a bit heavier than I expected, a long bronze blade that gradually grows into a sharpened point. Various curved symbols are carved into the metal, as well as the black crystal handle.

I step into the circle, practice swinging the sword to get used to the weight and balance. In a way I can't explain, holding and moving it feels oddly familiar, and natural. Acia and I touch swords before she gets into her stance.

"I'm gonna take it real easy, just try to copy what I'm doing alright."

I nod, positioning myself into her same stance. As we exchange the first few strikes, I can't help but feel as though I'm learning complicated choreography - mimicking her swings and foot movements while also blocking gentle jabs. Her white hair reflects the sun beautifully as the breeze from the ocean tosses it around. It's distracting almost, I can't help but feel a bit entranced by her soft features under the morning light.

A swift kick to my legs knocks me to the ground, and back to reality.

She stands over me, holding her hand out. "That was a good first go, just trust your reflexes a bit more. Don't hesitate"

I nod, taking her hand as she helps me up. I brush the sand off my T-shirt and pants, picking up my sword. "Let's go again, I can get this."

After about three different attempts to disarm Acia, I finally reach the point where I'm too exhausted to continue. I do feel much more comfortable overall with handling the weapon and protecting myself.

There's not much of a way to tell time here, I assume it's about noon when we all take a rest in the cool water. Small waves sweep against my ankles as I walk across the shoreline, eyes gazing over the distant horizon and endless ocean.

I hear splashing footsteps come up from behind as Acia catches up to walk beside me.
"So how are you doing?" She asks, brushing the hair from her face.
"Like, really. I know it's a lot to take in, we all had a hard time adjusting at first."

I nod, hands in my pockets. "Honestly, as crazy as it sounds, this is the best I've felt for a while. It wasn't the most-" I pause, kicking up the water in front of me.

"- healthy situation back at home. My foster family was beyond awful. I'm glad you were able to find me."

"It was Resmé who found you, she said you were basically leading us to you like a lighthouse when your powers showed up. I just tried to make sure you knew where to meet us."

"What's that like for you?" I ask, "Going into people's dreams I mean. It was almost like we'd met before."

"I've been able to since I was very young, that's how Resmé sensed me a while before the rest. I can't really explain how it works; I just go to different places when I dream. Sometimes I can feel people's memories and thoughts."

"So, you can hear what I'm thinking right now?" The idea understandably makes me a bit uncomfortable. She laughs, tightening her jean jacket as the breeze pushes against us.

"You don't have to worry about that, I usually just pick up on loud thoughts when I'm trying." She kicks a small bit of water at me.

"I do feel anxiousness coming off you though. I understand, but just know that we watch each other's backs here. You'll start feeling more natural soon."

She gestures to Seth walking alone in the water some distance in front of us. "-and don't pay him any attention. He's been a jealous mess since Resmé told us you were coming."

"Jealous of me? Why would he feel that way?"

Acia pauses.

"He's viewed himself as our leader since he got here a few years ago, only because he's the oldest. Now, he's just being reminded that he isn't meant to have that spot, you are."

"I don't know about being a leader, I just want to help where I can." I nod towards Seth's direction. "What's his story anyway, I'm guessing not too different from all of ours?"

Acia shrugs, brushing the hair from her face.

"As long as we've been here together, he hasn't mentioned much about his past. I know he's Canadian, and the only one of us to have a sibling - but he never talks about how he lost his family."

We hear Horace's bellowing voice call us from the far side of shore.

"It's time to head back," she says. "How do you feel about man-hunt?"

My head tilts curiously. "The game? I've never played before, why?"

She smiles, jabbing my shoulder playfully. "Oh, you're in for a treat today. C'mon, let's go."

*

Horace gathers us five in the circle once more, holding a soft-ball sized bright silver orb in his palm. It appears small compared to his large hands, curved grooves separating it into quadrants similar to a basketball.

"Firstly, I would like to avoid any injuries today,

if possible-" he begins, tossing the orb between his hands.

"For our newcomer, this training is meant to develop your speed, strength, and endurance."

Horace draws a long line in the sand with his boot, separating Acia and me from Felicia, Quinn, and Seth.

"Your goal is to place this orb on the stairs of the lake-house." he instructs, tossing the ball of silver over to me. "That is your most prized possession for the time being, protect it from these three as you navigate to the house."

He turns to their side of the line.
"We're here to grow and educate each other, please attempt to show some restraint." His eyes linger a bit longer on Seth while speaking.

"Protect yourselves, then we will begin." he says, gesturing towards bundles of armor in the sand.

We all strap the light metal pieces around our chest, arms and shoulders, alining ourselves on the beach according to Horace's instructions. Seth, Quinn, and Felicia ready their stances several yards behind me and Acia.

"How serious does this game get, exactly?" I laugh nervously, turning to Acia at my right.
She doesn't seem to return my lightheartedness.

"We can definitely get a bit...competitive here. Just try to stay close."

"Oh-" Is all I can say in return, my heart beginning to race. A mixture of both nerves and excitement.

"Ready yourselves-" Horace commands, holding a white cloth above his head.
As it glides gently to the ground, Acia and I sprint full speed ahead, somewhat unsteadily as the sand shifts beneath us. Unable to help looking back, I notice our three pursuers haven't left their places.

"We get a head start-" Acia says, pacing next to me. "Only thirty seconds, don't look back."

As we break through the slanted tree-line, I realize that I'm quickly falling behind her, despite pushing my legs to their limit. Her stride is graceful, and nimble as she dodges the tangled vines obstructing our path. Once she reaches several yards ahead of me within a second, it suddenly occurs to me that this amount of speed shouldn't be humanly possible. She slows her run as the gap of distance grows between us.

"You're trying too hard-" she says as I finally catch up to her.
"You need to run from here," she whispers, placing her hand against my pounding heart. "Not here." - touching a finger to my forehead. "Let your body move easily."

Her eyes lift sharply as there's the approaching sound of footsteps behind.

Quickly grabbing my hand, she more-or-less drags me behind her, matching my running pace. I secure the ball tightly under my arm as we gain speed.

Run from your heart. I tell myself, attempting to force thoughts of exhaustion away.

In the same way Resmé taught me, I try my best to clear all distractions - focusing only on the way ahead; the rushing wind against my skin, the beating of my own heart.

Incredibly, my aching legs begin to feel lighter, and the breeze blowing against me increases in intensity - as if we're moving on a rushing train. The trees ahead whip past at an amazing speed, although it seems as though my body knows to avoid every intercepting branch. I can see that I'm keeping up with Acia's strides, my brain unable to process what my body is now capable of.

From my peripheral, a flash of white suddenly bounds into view beside us. Quinn has caught up first, morphed into his terrifying panther form.
"This way!" Acia shouts over the rushing wind, making a sharp turn into the denser trees to our left.

I follow her closely as she jumps and turns evasively, my stomach churning as I see an abrupt stop to the ground in front of us approaching.
A wide river separates us from the other side of the forest, rushing water dashing against sharp, jagged rocks.

"We're going to have to jump." Acia yells, immediately sending my heart into my throat.

"Just trust me," she says, seemingly responding to my fear. "Trust yourself."

At her words, I will my legs to move even faster, carrying myself towards a feat that would've meant certain death a few days ago. We approach the sloped edge at full speed just as Quinn closes the distance between us, leaving no time to hesitate as I throw myself into the air.

Time seems to stand still as I soar over the violent flow of water fifty feet below, a vision from a dream. The sort of dream I'd jerk awake from just before hitting the ground.

I don't wake up, of course. Instead, the hard earth collides into my body as I severely miscalculate the landing. Momentum tosses me across the ground for several yards before coming to a painful stop.
With the wind knocked from my lungs, and pain radiating through my entire body, I still can't help but laugh internally realizing that I just threw myself past an angry ravine - and made it over alive.

"That could've turned out a better." laughs Acia as she kneels by my side.
"Bit of an understatement." I say, gripping my right shoulder as excruciating pulses surrounds my joint. "I

think it may be dislocated.

From ahead, I can see Felicia dashing toward us, Quinn pacing on the other side of the ravine.

"Give this to me," Acia says, rushing for the silver orb still clutched in my hands. "There's no time and you're hurt, I can get it to the house."

Defeated, I place the ball into her hands, wincing as my bone grinds against its socket.

"No Ethan!" exclaims Acia's voice, although it's surprisingly coming from Felicia's direction as she approaches us.

Suddenly, I realize.

As I look back up into Acia's face, the air around her distorts and shimmers like a mirage. The illusion fades away, Seth standing in front of me with the orb, a smug grin spread across his face.

"Taking candy from a baby." He says, tossing the orb to Felicia as she lands gracefully from across the ravine.

I see now that Acia was running to warn me, Seth replacing her image with Felicia's in my mind.

"I'm so sorry, I thought I saw you still running beside me." Says Acia as she approaches. "Are you alright?"

Felicia sets the orb on the ground, tenderly placing her hand against my shoulder.

"It'll need to be set." she says, turning to Acia & Seth. "Meet Horace back up at the house, I don't know if you'll want to be around for this."

A moment after both of them head up the grassy slope, Felicia gently helps me remove the armor from my torso. Picking up a thin nearby branch, she snaps off a small piece.

"You'll want to bite down on this, believe me."

I brace myself, clenching down on the perfume-flavored twig as she places my shoulder between her hands. The warm golden glow spreads from her palms into my skin, instantly beginning to calm the pain.
But the moment is short-lived.

"One..." she counts, although abandoning the remaining numbers. An immense pressure and grinding sensation shoots through my arm as she slips my joint

161

back into its socket, sending an uncontrollable shout through my gritted teeth.

"That sucked - really sucked." I wince, my uncomfortable laugh distorted from pain.

"Which is why I asked them to leave." She nods understandingly. "Thought you might need some space."

As her hands move from my shoulder, the unbearable pain subsides. I rotate my arm hesitantly, feeling no discomfort whatsoever.

"Five stars doc." I smile, "Second time you've put me back together. I appreciate you, really."

Felicia smiles sheepishly, brushing her two long braids behind her back.

"It's what I do." She holds out her hand to help me up.

"Let's head back, I'm starving."

*

After a fresh meal of greens and strawberries from Felicia's garden and a warm bath, I'm finally able to retreat to my room to rest. As I lie there, staring at the wooden beams in the ceiling and replaying all the sights from today, I can't ignore the feeling that I'm starting to not recognize myself. Not in a bad way, but I've adopted an entirely different story for my life in only a couple of days.

Does this all seem impossibly surreal? Most definitely. But despite the new fears and burdens to come, I would never consider returning to my old life.

It isn't long before my eyelids become heavy, and I plunge into a deep sleep.

Chapter Eleven

*U*nlike many times before, I am aware of the moment I begin dreaming. Suddenly, I find myself walking on a pearly white beach under silvery blue moonlight, with waves crashing against large boulders along the shoreline. To my right, there's a thick forest of ginormous tropical trees, suggesting that this might be an island of some kind. It doesn't seem to be Earth, as two large moons illuminate the night sky.

I instinctively approach one of the trees and place my hand on its smooth trunk, realizing these trees must be thousands of years old, given that it would take about sixty seconds to walk around the thick base of the trunk.

A glint of light catches my eye from several yards in the darkness. Strangely, I feel as though I'm gently being pulled towards it. As I step further into the shadows of the huge leaves above, I'm astonished as the thick blanket of trees begins to separate, forming a path. They move smoothly, as if the ground is made of shallow water, settling into a neat walkway that guides me towards the mysterious light. I hesitantly tread in its direction, ensuring the path doesn't close behind me.

After two minutes of walking, I observe the source of the light—a shimmering blue lagoon. A waterfall gently pours from the curved cave-like structure surrounding it. The glowing light, dancing through the water, seems to radiate from deep in its center. Without a second thought, I start walking towards it, the pull moving my legs before I can fully register.

As the cold water reaches my waist, I can feel the rocky surface under my feet abruptly end.

Sinking down like a stone, I'm unable to see clearly except for the light source cutting through the cloudiness. Trying my best to swim towards it, I realize that my body is so heavy that I'm unable to push myself through the water. I begin sinking faster and faster, the air in my lungs forced out by the freezing pressure. The further I sink, the brighter the light grows. There are incredibly long vines of sea plants surrounding me, waving through the water like menacing tentacles. The source of the light seems to be a round object at the bottom of the lagoon floor. Although I'm unable to directly see it through the intense glow, I can just make out the shapes of stone pillars and an algae covered stone surface.

Before I can reach the pool's bottom, the light suddenly fades away like a flame in the wind. Chilling shadows immediately swallow me whole, the only light coming from the distant moon above the water's surface. Attempting to kick my way back up to air, I feel the vines tangling around my legs and arms, and panic begins to set in. I try my hardest to jerk my eyes open, attempting to wake myself up, but it continues to fail.

Abruptly, there's a motion in the water, as if something darted in front of me. I stop flailing my arms and remain completely still, exerting all effort to discern what lurks in my surroundings. As I grow dizzy from the lack of oxygen, a pair of narrow red eyes emerge in the darkness, glaring at me intensely with a low hiss echoing through the water.

Just as the creature lunges towards me, I'm snatched from the dream and back into my room, still struggling to get a single breath.

Water heaves from my mouth as I sit up on my bed; an unnatural amount, as if I'd actually been drowning. Gasping for air, I grip my sheets, realizing that I'm entirely drenched, and so is my mattress.

Stumbling onto the floor, there's a loud splash as I step into ankle-depth water. *What the hell is happening?*

Every inch of my room is dripping wet- the windows, walls, even the ceiling. Before I can reach the door to call for
help, it flings open from the outside. All the trapped water rushes out like a stream into the hallway, nearly knocking over Resmé as she stands at the door holding a lantern.

"Oh goodness, are you okay child?" She waves her hand over the floor and walls. Just as miraculously as it had appeared, the water dissolves into clouds of mist and vanishes without a trace.

"I don't know what happened," I say, tears streaming down my face from the coughing fit. "I was having a dream, or at least I thought it was. I must've drawn in the water by accident."

Resmé places her palm on my forehead, closing her eyes for a moment.

"It was not a dream, but a vision." She stammers, opening her eyes and taking my hands. "I recognize this place, the two moons. You were shown Cephris, a planet far outside of this universe."

I replay images from the dream in my head - the feeling of being pulled towards the light-source in the water.

"There was something glowing in this lagoon that kept drawing me in, I don't know what it was, I just felt that it was important."

Resmé's face appears almost frightened as I envision the shadowy creature again, as if she's watching the memory along with me.

"The further your power expands, the closer the shadows will grow. They can sense that you've located an emblem."

"Is that what was at the bottom of the water? Are you sure what I saw was real?"

Resmé places her hand on my shoulder.
"The emblems are beginning to call you as their guardian. We'll prepare to gather the first one immediately."

Chapter Twelve

As I consider the daunting task of searching for this mysterious object, I can't help but acknowledge how utterly unprepared I am. In truth, I'm still grappling with the surrealism of this entirely new world and the unexpected situation I've been thrust into. Resmé, however, shows no hesitation and promptly rouses the others in the house to gather in the dining room. Their expressions lack enthusiasm, understandably so, given that it's the middle of the night and the abrupt interruption to their sleep.

"The time has finally come," she begins after everyone is seated around the table. "An emblem has revealed itself to Ethan, hidden on the distant world

Cephris. We'll be leaving by sunset tomorrow to allow for rest, such a far journey may be strenuous."

The table is quiet for a moment as Quinn, Acia, Felicia and Seth exchange concerned looks.
"Do you really think we're ready?" Quinn asks, voice shaking, "I knew that it would be soon since he got here, just not this soon."

"We don't have a choice." Seth says flatly, "If they're ready to be found, that means the end is getting closer."

"No Seth, there's always a choice." Horace interrupts as he leans against the doorway. "Anyone who wishes to stay here may do so if you're frightened, but this is what you've been training for."

"Of course, we would never force you into danger," says Resmé, "But Seth is right, the end *is* growing nearer. I can feel the prison dimension tearing open every passing day. It's best to move together while we still can."

Felicia stands from her seat, looking around the table.

"We're not afraid, we've been here hiding for too long, guys. Once this is over, we can live in the real world again."

"Assuming we're not killed before then." Seth sighs, leaning back in his chair.

"You're always so negative, just give it a rest, would you?" Acia snaps, narrowing her eyes at him before turning to Resmé.

"Is the world deserted? Or should we be prepared for whatever's living there."

"I never knew of living creatures on Cephris, but much can change in several millennia. We will be cautious."

*

I stare up into the ceiling once again, unable to close my eyes to sleep. Tomorrow promises a deeper plunge into this surreal journey, and I can't shake the mental images of terrifying creatures and lurking dangers in this other world.

The drum of my racing heartbeat fills my ears in the silent darkness. I wrap the pillow around my head to try to drown out the sound, forcing myself to breathe slowly. *'It will be okay.'* I whisper, *'I will be okay'*. There's a sudden tap at my bedroom doorway.

"Hey, are you awake in there?" Says Acia's voice softly.

I get up from bed to open the door.

"You know it, I can't sleep at all. Same for you I'm guessing?"

She nods, shrugging her shoulders. "Just a bit excited really. Maybe a few nerves thrown in there." I notice she's wearing her jean jacket and sneakers, not exactly what you'd wear to sleep.

"I'm going on a little walk near the wall, since we may not be back here in a while."

"The wall?" I ask, "Where is that?"

She raises an eyebrow, "I'm surprised Resmé hasn't shown it to you yet. Stick on your shoes, you're coming with me."

I smile, grateful for her helping me to escape my own anxious episode. I throw on my boots and old hoodie, following Acia quietly down the stairs and through the front door. She leads me into the forest behind the house, walking so quickly I have to put in some effort to keep up. The swaying light from her lantern helps me to avoid tripping over the protruding roots in the ground.

"So…" I begin breathlessly, "What kind of place is this? An Island or something else? Resmé told me we're inside of a pocket dimension, but I haven't asked more questions."

"You'll see in a second." is all she responds with, not slowing her pace. I'm feeling a bit more excited the further we go into the tightly packed trees.
Before long, the sound of crashing waves echoes in the distance. As we finally reach past the tree line, I see we're on a towering cliff with the shimmering ocean stretching ahead.

Approaching the very edge of the cliff, she picks up a small rock and turns it between her fingers.

"This place is a lot smaller than it looks." She says, reaching back to throw the stone. It flies several yards over the edge before suddenly bouncing against an invisible barrier. There's a loud ringing through the air as blue ripples appear where the rock had struck, as if the small patch of sky were made of water. The ripples spread up and outwards, distorting the view of the ocean and stars before settling.

"Is all of this some kind of hologram?" I ask, perplexed as I watch the rock fall into the water far below.

"Think pocket dimension, like you said before." Acia responds, tucking her jacket around her as the wind picks up.

"It's oval shaped, we're towards the back end now, closest to the wall. There's nothing outside of the barrier, Resmé and Horace are the only ones who can bridge between here and the real world."

"Doesn't that make you feel trapped?" I ask, quickly realizing it probably sounds a bit dumb under the circumstances we're in.

"Not exactly, I feel the safest I've ever been before. Most of us have seen some terrible things on the outside."

I pause for a moment, before asking my next question. "If it's okay to talk about, what happened before Resmé brought you here?"

She turns back to the ocean, picking up another rock to throw.

"My father knew about my powers since I was a little kid. There's not many Esparethians that remember their heritage, but my family did. They were terrified."

Acia hurls another stone into the barrier, almost throwing herself off balance.

"He knew that eventually Asdroth would come after me, and him. So, he abandoned me in his mountain cabin thinking it might keep me hidden."

My heart falls into my stomach for her, I never thought that she may have been deserted as well. I gently place my hand on her shoulder, struggling to find the words for a moment.

"I'm sorry that happened to you, I can't imagine how scary that must've been."

Acia turns to walk towards the forest again, I follow close behind.

"I was only there alone for a week before the shades were able to find me. I almost didn't survive." Holding the lantern to her side, she lifts her shirt slightly to reveal a long scar across her ribs. I gasp, wincing as I realize such a large gash had to come from something wide and razor sharp.

"Before they could kill me, Resmé appeared and transported me here. I haven't seen or heard of my father since, not that it bothers me."

As we come back into the stretch of open land where the house sits, Acia and I take a seat by the lake's edge. The reflection of the star-studded night sky gently swirls in the breeze as we sit in silence. I look over to her as the moonlight reflects off her silvery hair, eyes drawn up to the stars. I realize this is the first time in a while I've been able to interact with someone as a friend, even if it hasn't been for very long.

"So, what's your story? You don't really talk about yourself much." Acia asks, resting her chin on her palm as she turns towards me.

I open my mouth to answer, but I'm not sure where to begin. The events from my past aren't something I try to revisit often.

"There's not much of a story really. I was passed between foster homes most of my life, I don't remember much of anything before then."

"So, you don't remember your parents? Or anything about your life before?"

"Not clearly, I just remember living with different strangers. I was left in front of an Orphanage in Jersey as a baby."

Acia nods slowly, looking down for a moment.

"What happened when you first used your powers? Were you afraid?"

I look out into the lake, remembering the moment in the cellar when the orb of light first appeared. Remembering how Harold Dunkle's charred arm looked after he beat me with the rod. I can't help but wonder what they may have done after I left that awful house. My stomach sinks with guilt as I remember the sound of the ambulance rushing by as I hid in the trees.

"It's okay," Acia says gently, taking my hand in her own.

"You don't have to talk about it, I can feel it. It must've been awful going through all of that."

My heart beats a bit faster as I feel the warmth of her hand, I immediately hope she doesn't notice.

"I didn't realize what was happening, but it appeared when I needed it to. Resmé is helping me to learn control, I think it's starting to work."

I look down at her smooth hand, tenderly cupped over mine. As my eyes draw up to meet hers, I become lost for a moment, as if everything around me disappears except for her gaze. My breath catches, heartbeat rising into my throat.

In all the books I've read and shows I've seen, this is what I had imagined it would feel like when beginning to fall for someone. It may sound ridiculous, given it's only been a few days, but there's something in her deep, silvery eyes that's inexplicably comforting yet intimidating. Her mouth curves into a slight smile, her eyes leaving mine and turning towards the water.

"Uhm, Ethan?" She laughs nervously, letting go of my hand.

"What's wrong?" I ask, glancing towards the lake as well. A gasp escapes once I see what caught her attention.

Waving above the lake's surface are hundreds of large droplets of water, flowing upwards from the lake as if gravity has suddenly reversed.

I stand up quickly, approaching the water's edge to get a closer view. As a droplet floats towards me, I reach out to grasp it. It bursts in my hand, drenching my face and clothes. As I stumble backwards, all the other floating droplets splash back into the water.

Acia laughs and claps her hands as I stand dripping wet.

"Did you do that on purpose?"
I laugh with her, staring confusingly at the water.

"I have a lot more to learn than I realize."

I twist the cold water from my T-shirt, shaking out my wet hair.

"I think that may be a sign to head in for the night." I laugh, nodding toward the house. "We're going to need some kind of rest for tomorrow."

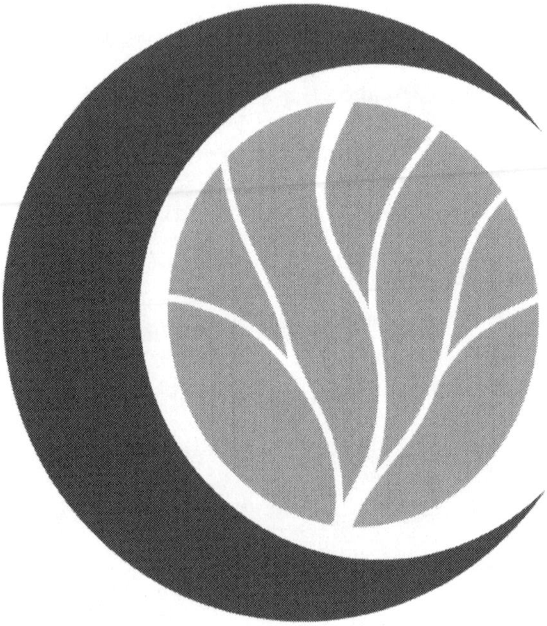

Chapter Thirteen

"This is the most disgusting thing I've ever eaten." Quinn gags as we sit around the breakfast table, spitting into a cloth napkin.

"Just try to suck it up, they're supposed to help with the travel sickness." Says Felicia, grinning a bit.

I look down at my bowl of the twisted green roots, hesitating as I pick one up. "What did you say these were called again?"

"Epsire roots, I've been growing them for a year. Unless you feel like puking up your guts later, I would try to eat them."

As my mind flashes back to how sick I became when I first landed here, I start chewing on the root right away.

It's incredibly bitter and tough, nearly forcing its way back up as I swallow.

"You're crazy man." Laughs Quinn as he watches my disgusted expression. "I'll take my chances with the puke later."

He stands from the table, picking up an apple from the middle before walking towards the door. "I'm heading to the weapons shed if anyone wants to join me."

"I'll take you up on that." I say while still chewing, standing up from my spot.

"I'll be there in a bit, just waiting for Acia to come downstairs." Says Felicia as she waves us on.

I notice it's colder outside than it has been for the last few days, much colder. The sky is filled with thick clouds casting a shadow over the entire stretch of land. Quinn looks up curiously.

"Weird, I can't remember the last time I've seen it rain here." He says, continuing to walk towards the rear of the house. Surrounded by a tangle of vines and branches is an old wooden shed, leaning slightly from the age of the frame. My breath catches a bit as Quinn opens the double-sided doors revealing an array of weapons hanging on the shed walls. Curiously shaped swords, bows, axes, staffs and shields reflect the light streaming in through cracks in the walls. Carved into the metal of the blades and arrowheads are the same symbols I've seen etched into the training circle.

"Could you tell me what these symbols mean? Or what they're for." I ask as I pick up a blade from the wall, running my finger across the carved grooves.

"Horace says our people created them during the first war, infusing symbols with protection magic. Any weapon without them can't kill a shade, aside from our powers." He picks up an ax, flipping it around in his palm.

It's odd seeing a kid my age casually handling weapons like this. Still, I suppose it's much less strange than seeing a human transform into an extremely large animal.

"If it's okay for me to ask, what's it like when you change?" I say hesitantly as he straps a belt of knives around his waist.

"It's…complicated. A bit uncomfortable, almost hurts but not as much as it used to when I was younger. The thing is, I don't remember much after I shift back to human form. It's two completely different sides."

"Reminds me of those old werewolf movies. Sounds pretty cool honestly - if it's alright for me to say that."

I slip a black leather sword holster from a hook in the wall, strapping it around my waist before slipping my blade into it.

"Believe me, I used to hate my life until I could control the change. It wasn't so pretty dealing with it back at home, I even had to live alone in the woods for a while. This place really saved my life."

I try to mentally picture the image of a huge white panther leaping through the trees in a Miami forest, or community.

"Do you think it'll be hard to get back to a normal life after all of this is over? Most of you have been growing up here for a while."

We walk from the shed and towards the front of the house.

"I'm not even sure there will be a normal after all of this is over man. I know it's hard to wrap your head around it since all we've seen is training, but we're about to see a lot of scary stuff once we step out of here. I don't know if living a quiet life is possible after that."

His words add more twists to my already queasy stomach. I know that he's probably right, PTSD is a burden many people take home with them from war. But the delusional part of me isn't ready to accept the fear of what will happen once our mission is over. I must force my mind to stay in this present moment. Two loud thuds pull me from my thoughts.

Quinn walks over to the large tree he just flung knives into, pulling them out firmly.

"I'm guessing you've never thrown one of these, do you want to try?"

For about half an hour he shows me how to properly throw a knife several yards. It takes that entire time for me to finally get the blade to strike the tree trunk. As I go to retrieve it, there's a sudden sinking feeling in the pit of my stomach.

Inexplicably, my body feels as though it's in danger, my heart beginning to race although nothing around me has changed. There isn't a sound from the deep forest in front of me, not even a leaf rustling in the wind.

"What's up dude?" Quinn asks as he sees me frozen in place.

My eyes scan the trees, still seeing nothing. "Something's not right, I'm not sure what it is."

A shadow falls over us along with a cold gust of wind as the dark gray clouds spread across the sky. The air smells and feels like it usually does right before a heavy storm.

"You said it's never rained here before, right?"

Quinn nods nervously, scratching his head. The house door swings open as Resmé steps out onto the porch, her eyes looking up into the sky. A concerned frown forms on her face.

"Do you feel that too?" I ask while approaching her place on the stairs.

She closes her eyes while facing upwards into the clouds, flinging them back open.

"Both of you, come with me." Raising her hands, I feel the earth shift under my feet as the house and all other surroundings dissolve away in a violent rush of wind.

Once my eyes adjust, I see we're standing on a cliff which oversees the shoreline. The rolling storm clouds stretch far over the horizon, appearing almost black in the furthest part.

"I'm afraid we'll have to depart sooner than planned." Resmé gasps, showing a fearful expression I couldn't have imagined on her face.

Thunder rumbles through the air so strongly I can feel it in my chest.

"What's happening Resmé?" Quinn asks, unable to hide the shaking in his voice.

Before she can answer, powerful bolts of lightning strike the forest close behind us. Almost immediately after, we can see smoke and the glow of flames rising high above the branches.

Quinn takes off running towards it, despite my call after him. I sprint the short distance into the trees before we come to the clearing where fire is spreading. What neither of us expect to see is a figure already waiting inside of the tall red flames.

*

The fire is contained somehow in the outline of a circle, encasing a narrow silhouette kneeling in its center.

"Seth?" Shouts Quinn in shock. "Seth, what the hell is happening?"

Seth's darkened eyes rise from the ground to stare blankly at us, his pupils reflecting the blaze. His mouth widens slowly into a menacing grin as he stands to his feet. "You've all been such idiots- entirely pathetic. I don't think you realize how much I'll enjoy this."

Within an instant of hearing his words, I know in my heart that all of the negative gut feelings I've had towards Seth, were not without reason. This look in his eyes is one of pure hatred, as if he's just been waiting on the opportunity to unmask a facade and reveal his truest self. I don't know how it hasn't been as clear until now.

Resmé suddenly appears between Quinn and I, immediately taken aback. Her gaze falls to the various sharp symbols etched into the ground beneath him.

"What have you done-" She rages past us, charging towards Seth furiously.

"What have you done!" With a great amount of strength, she throws her hand at the flames, sending a powerful burst of wind tearing through the circle.

Holding his hands up defensively, Seth seemingly shields the fire completely from Resmé's efforts.

"You're too late, you old hag." He spits, the whites of his eyes shifting into an inky black. Stretching his arms wide, the fire surrounding him expands towards us in a scorching wave.

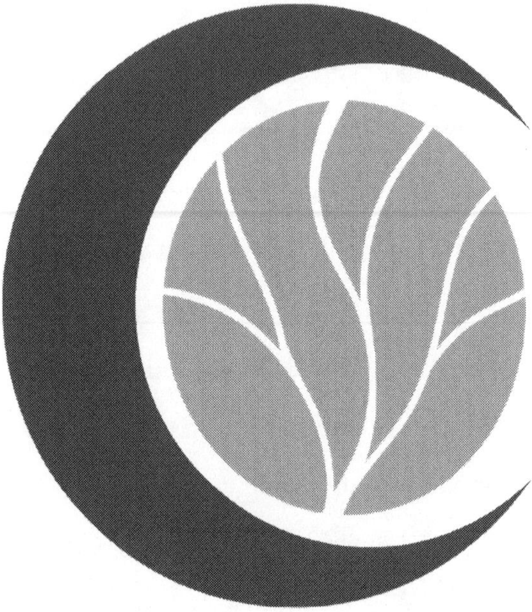

Chapter Fourteen

*A*n intense force knocks the air from my lungs as I'm flung to the ground several yards away. Through my blurred vision, I see the circle of fire has doubled in size, the scorching heat burning my skin as Seth continues to raise his arms to the sky.

The dark clouds above swirl as if a tornado is beginning to form, separating at the center to reveal a black patch of sky. The darkness draws my eyes deep into it, a pillar of black mist beginning to descend directly over us.

As a hand firmly grasps my shoulder, the earth shifts under me once again in a jarring wave of wind and colors. We're in front of the house once more, Resmé standing over me and Quinn.

"He's betrayed us all, we must leave this place immediately."

"Those symbols, the circle -" Quinn realizes, "What is he trying to summon Resmé?"

She pulls us towards the house, looking back nervously at the darkness.

"He's drawn servants of darkness here to us, I don't understand how I couldn't sense his intentions long ago."

Half a mile away now, the swirling pillar of black mist has touched the forest. Almost immediately, the trees closest begin to wither and lose the color from their leaves, a wave of death spreading outward like a flame to paper.

As the trees near us also begin to turn, a bitter cold breeze pushes through the naked branches.

There's a shrill scream from inside of the house, followed by Felicia calling for Resmé in a panicked voice. We all rush into the house and up the staircase, following Felicia's voice into Acia's room. She kneels beside the bed as Acia lies motionless, clutching her stiff hand. Her eyelids remain open, although there is only glossy blackness where the whites of her eyes should be. Resmé rushes to her side, placing the palm of her hand over her forehead.

"Seth has linked her to his spell" She cries, voice quivering. "- he's draining her life force to pierce the barrier."

My eyes fall to Acia's wrists and arms. There's multiple of the same strange symbols written on her skin that were etched in Seth's circle.

"The symbols on her arms, can you remove them?"

Resmé looks up at me. "What symbols do you see? Where are they?"

I walk over to kneel beside her, gently holding Acias left arm.

"You don't see these?"

The moment my hands touch her skin, there's a warm glow that spreads from my palms into her arm. I immediately let go, unsure of what may have happened. Within an instant, I see the symbols dissolving from her skin on both arms as the warm glow spreads across her body. The inky black color fades from her eyes before they close gently.

"What just happened?" Felicia asks, staring at me blankly.

"The link's been cut, but I couldn't see the source of the spell." Resmé looks at me, bewildered. "Could you feel what kind of dark forces Seth is using against us?"

I shake my head, wringing my hands. "I'm not sure what happened, that wasn't on purpose at all."

Through the bedroom window we can see that the swirling patch of black sky has begun to shrink in size. However, the dark clouds remaining are still stretching towards us. Resmé rises quickly. "Where is Horace, have any of you seen him?"

Quinn, Felicia and I look at each other shaking our heads. I haven't seen him since yesterday, which usually wouldn't seem abnormal considering he tends to isolate when not training.

"Seth has to be drawing energy from somewhere else to maintain the connection, Horace must be -"

"-Hey guys…" Quinn interrupts, pointing out of the window. "That looks like something we should be concerned about."

Across the lake the forest has begun to rumble, the trees swaying as if a large stampede of animals is rushing through them.

"There's no time. Outside, now." Resmé says, picking up Acia from the bed. "You all must leave before me, I have to find Horace. If he's been spelled, Seth could be using him as another anchor."

"No way," argues Felicia, "We're as good as dead without you. We have to stay here until you find him."

"You all cannot stay here, it is too late. Death will be upon us at any moment now."

We race down the stairs and out through the front door, Felicia scrambling to collect her bow and quiver of arrows from a hook on the wall.

The rumbling in the trees across the lake has ceased, but I can sense something in the tree's shadows, reminiscent of countless nightmares I've had before.

The only sound is the wind howling through the branches and my own heartbeat. A lump rises into my throat, fist clenching.

"You're more than capable Ethan," Resmé whispers, carefully placing Acia in Quinn's arms. "Reach from within, command your surroundings."

She grabs my shoulders firmly. "I'm leaving you all with a gift, the best protection I can give to you now-"

She reaches under the outer layer of her gray gown, pulling out a short knife. Swiftly, she makes a long cut across the surface of her own palm, causing us all to wince. As a trickle of blood runs from between her fingers, she waves her hand in a circular motion, speaking in a complicated, decorative language I'm unable to understand.

Incredibly, a blue glow begins to appear underneath the earth where the blood has landed. The energy grows in intensity and stretches out towards the four of us, encircling the area around our feet. The light's pattern resembles a tree, beginning at Resmé's feet and branching out in our separate directions.

    I'm completely still as the light bleeds from the ground onto my legs, creating a warm, staticky sensation. My limbs and torso grow heavier as the light scales my body, the feeling of fitted fabric appearing against my skin. Once the swirling glow fades, I'm able to see what it left behind.

    All four of us now stand donned in sleek, obsidian-black armor. Numerous separate panels composing its surface curve around my body organically, the obsidian-black shell reflecting the last remnants of sunlight. Resmé looks around at all of our surprised, and terrified faces.

    "It will all be well, you all are stronger than you realize. Now please, run!"

We all exchange nervous glances for a fleeting moment, then simultaneously start running toward the forest on the right side of the lake. Glancing back briefly, I notice Resmé has vanished in a flash of silver.

Quinn, a bit behind Felicia and me, carries Acia over his shoulder. My heart continues to pound in my ears as the forest line steadily approaches.

"Wait!" Quinn yells just before we enter the tree's shadows.

Felicia and I stop in our tracks.

"Do you hear that?" He says, his head turned sharply to the left.

Our eyes scan the left side of the forest across the lake, the trees have begun to sway once again.

My heart seemingly stops beating as a long spindly arm extends from the darkness into the open. The towering body that follows appears thin and sharply angled, with nearly every bone protruding from its gray, leathery skin. Hunching on all fours in a predator's stance, its piercing red eyes cut across the stretch of land, locking onto mine.

"Shades."

Quinn and Felicia breathlessly say almost in unison. "We're dead, we're dead." Quinn stutters, bending under the weight of Acia on his shoulder.

More of the creatures timidly step from the forest line, moving in a way that makes me believe they're hesitant.

"Why are they moving that way, what are they waiting for." I ask myself, although Felicia answers.

"They need the shadows, can't step into the light."

I notice the shrinking strip of daylight which separates the halves of the lake. The darkening clouds threaten to remove our protection at any moment.

My eyes fall to the water as it tosses in the wind.

"Reach from within, command your surroundings." Resmé's voice echoes in my ears.

A blood curdling screech slices through the air as the shades begin tearing across the open land towards us. Only a thin strip of sunlight remains before them.

"Go, now!" I tell Quinn and Felicia as I force my legs towards the lake.

"Ethan what the hell are you doing, we need to leave!" Felicia yells, although it falls to deaf ears. I charge headlong at a breathtaking speed towards the wave of terrifying creatures, my heart pounding like a relentless jackhammer against the armor.

As I reach the edge of the water, my hands stretch out to the lake with all my might.

I unleash the pent-up fear and suppressed emotions from within me, propelling them forcefully through the palms of my hands - commanding the waters to move.

A thunderous shockwave erupts from my body, racing across the lake's surface and sucking the air from my chest. The weight of the water bears down through my arms and hands as I force the waves to rise, converging into a single, swirling pillar.

Shades, their shrieks escalating, creep along the outer edge of the lake, drawing closer to our side. Summoning every ounce of strength, I strenuously hurl my arms, propelling the viciously swirling water into the heart of the approaching swarm. As their bodies thrash and struggle against the strong current, I 'm struggling to maintain the field of water around them.

A deep pain and pressure begins to crush around my chest.

I can't breathe.

Darkness bleeds around the corners of my eyes, the ground violently swaying as I fall to my knees.

"Please, not now." I plead with myself, begging my body to regain strength. But it's no use, my arms fall to the ground, causing the tons of water to crash to the earth and away from the shades.

My heart plummets to the bottom of my stomach as they rise from the ground, roaring in furious anger. It's at this moment that I can discern their horrifying faces, or the unsettling lack thereof.

The shape of their heads is disturbingly human, leathery skin tightly bound to the sharp angles of their skulls. Devoid of eyes, ears, or any facial features, except for wide rows of razor-sharp teeth stretching from ear to ear.

As my vision begins to return, I realize with horror that a few of them have recovered faster than the others, only several yards remaining between us.

I draw the sword from my side, struggling to force my legs to stand. The only choices left are to run, fight, or die. Considering my limbs can't cooperate at this moment, I suppose only the third option is feasible. I grip the handle of the long blade, facing the towering creatures as they tear across the ground on all fours with their long-hooked claws.

I dodge quickly as the first one attempts to ram its body into mine, slashing their claws against my armored back.

I whip my sword in defense instinctively, leaping into the air while slashing into its leathery arm. From this proximity, I can swell a sickeningly sweet oder emanating from its skin.

The creature barely reacts to the wound, powerfully knocking its sharpened elbow into my chest. Flying backwards several yards, I land harshly onto the wet earth, my armor absorbing a great deal of the impact.

Suddenly, there's a whistling over my head as an arrow flies directly into the skull of my attacker.

It collapses to the ground, releasing a vibrating wail as it attempts to claw the arrow from its head. Its skin radiates like hot iron around the wound, a flow of steaming black blood pouring onto the grass. Another silver arrow sinks into the throat of the next creature, followed by one to its chest.

  I turn to see Felicia running towards me while loading another arrow into her bow. Quinn is close beside her, suddenly leaping several feet into the air and bursting into his white panther form. He outpaces her in a few bounds and halts in front of me, lifting under my body with his head so that I roll over onto his back. I force myself to sit upright, holding tightly to the long fur around his neck.

  He turns and rushes towards Felicia just as the remaining Shades overtake us, nearly throwing me backwards with how astoundingly fast we're moving. I reach out to grab Felicia's outstretched hand, pulling her onto Quinn's back in one single motion.

  As we bound towards the forest, I see Acia struggling to prop herself against a tree. Felicia sends more arrows flying behind us before reaching out to pull her onto Quinn's back.

Despite his speed, the shades are nearly overtaking us as we bound through the shadows, dodging in between scattered trees.

They leap into the branches overhead, the sound of their screeches echoing above us. As one nearly slashes Quinn's hind legs, Felicia outstretches her hand towards it, her palm glowing with bright red energy.

Within an instant, the shade crumbles to the ground, its body withering like an old forgotten flower. Only now do I realize Felicia's true power; life force manipulation. She chooses to heal, but also carries the touch of death.

From that display of power, she is suddenly visually fatigued, her nose bleeding as she tries to steady herself.

Gathering my strength once again, I turn and reach my hand towards the speedily approaching shades, silently speaking one word in my mind as I visualize flames consuming their bodies.

"Burn."

It takes only a moment to realize that I've made a terrible mistake as the branches and leaves above burst into flames, sending a massive heat wave washing over us. The shades begin to crash down as their bodies set ablaze, causing Quinn to dodge around frantically as sparks fly all around. Many are still able to avoid the burning branches, although we gain some distance from them. The fire rapidly jumps onto the path in front of us and spreads in all directions.

"Ethan, you have to stop, it's spreading too fast!" yells Felicia over the roar of the flames.

But despite how hard I try to calm them, my mind and body feel beyond strained and empty. I have nothing left.

Just as we're becoming overwhelmed by the heat, there seems to be a clearing in front of us. I quickly recognize it as the cliff Resmé & I have visited only days before.

"Quinn, we have to find another way, or we'll drop off!" I yell, holding tightly around Acia.

"There isn't another way," she says unsteadily, "The cave is close; we'll just have to swim."

My heart sinks. Hitting the water from such a height...I have doubts that we'd survive.

The blood curdling screeches behind remind me that we have no other choice.

Quinn doesn't slow his speed as the cliff comes into full view. I take one last glance behind us at the dozens of creatures leaping from tree to tree as fire eats at their flesh; an image that will forever be burned into my thoughts.

Gravity suspends for a moment as Quinn vaults from the ledge, just barely dodging the claws of a Shade that jumps in pursuit of us.

The sensation of free-falling from several hundred feet in the air is something from my greatest fears. I've dissociated from my body to avoid the pure shock of rushing towards the crashing waves, unsure if jagged rocks await us at the bottom.

Just as I squeeze my eyes tightly shut to prepare for impact, there's a sudden shift in gravity as I feel myself turn right side up.

Opening my eyes, I see that we're on the beach sand, Resmé kneeling in front of us. She's extremely fatigued, a long bleeding gash across her cheek. Felicia rushes up to embrace her.

"You're alright, thank goodness."

"We won't be for much longer, come now." She says, gesturing to the cave opening near us.

More shades have leapt from the cliff and begun swimming towards shore, cutting through the water like snakes. Quinn struggles to stand, now melting into his human form - completely exhausted. Resmé drapes his arm around her before we run across the sand, clinging tightly to a brown leather satchel strapped across her shoulder.

Where's Horace?

What could be so important in that bag that she would leave us to go back for it?

As we near the mouth of the cave, there's a sinister stir in the darkness. We find ourselves frozen in horror as two towering shades materialize, crawling slowly on all fours. Their wide mouths curve into a malevolent grin as an eerie stillness envelops them, punctuated by throaty clicking noises as if they're suppressing an insatiable urge to attack. From the shadows emerges another hooded figure, slowly wringing his hands together,

"Why are you doing this Seth, what have we done to deserve your betrayal?" Resmé demands, her voice carrying more guttural pain than anger. She draws her sword from her waist.

He only smiles, raising two of his fingers in the air. Suddenly, I feel as if liquid fire has begun to spread under my skin. I'm forced to the ground by the unimaginable pain, my teeth sinking into my bottom lip, drawing the taste of iron. Through my blurred vision, I see we've all collapsed.

"Power, freedom from your prophecies." He says eerily calmly, stepping over to Resmé as she writhes on the ground. He draws his sword and presses the tip into her back.

"Once you all are dead, and the emblems are destroyed, I'll be ruling my own part of the world, as I should. My own oasis. What have you ever offered me?" He flimsily waves his blade over in my direction.

"The only one of us promised anything was him." He crouches slowly beside me, lowering his voice to a sinister whisper.

"All of the power, right? Where's that power now.?"

Chapter Fifteen

My heart burns like a wildfire, each beat sending fiery pulses through my veins. Inside my mind, I'm screaming at the top of my lungs, yet no sound can escape my lips.

Seth raises his sword, preparing to strike Resmé's neck. I feel another surge of raw power and anger flowing through me. With all the strength I have left, I stretch the palm of my hand towards him.

A torrent of energy courses through my entire body, sending a beam of golden light hurtling towards Seth's chest. The light strikes him with tremendous force, his black cloak bursting into dripping, wet flames. He's thrown back into the cave wall with enough impact to crack the stone.

Not wasting a moment, my other hand reaches out towards the two Shades attempting to retreat into the darkness.

But Felicia and Acia have already taken action. With her glowing hand outstretched, Felicia once again causes the shade to painfully wither to the grown, Acia throwing her sword into the head of her opponent with frightening accuracy.

I quickly help Resmé to her feet and pick up her leather satchel, Quinn wrapping her other arm over his shoulder for support. Seth lies writhing on the ground, completely enveloped in flames as he tries to peel the melted cloak fabric from his skin.

More shrieks can be heard behind us as shades reach the beach, along with others cutting through the water. Felicia sends arrows flying over my head before we race into the shadows of the cave. The horrifying sounds of the approaching shades echo against the walls, accompanied by our labored breathing.

"Step back for a moment." orders Resmé, struggling to stand as she pulls away from Quinn and I. She stretches her trembling hands towards the deepest part of the cave, uttering another string of ancient unintelligible words.

"Ethan, we're going to need some cover - like, right now." panics Quinn, his eyes widening in fear as the shades tear across the sand towards us.

Without hesitation, I visualize and manifest a wall of fire once again, completely sealing off the cave entrance.

Flickering shadows dance along the walls, intense heat causing a band of sweat to form on our foreheads. As Resmé continues to speak in this mysterious language, a circle of glowing blue symbols begin to form around us.

A strong gust of wind flows around the cave, tossing up the sand and creating a small cyclone. The ground beneath us begins to shift and sway, the cave's walls distorting as each stone dissolves into a swirling colorful mist.

Acia's hand slips into mine as a feeling of weightlessness envelops us, the last of the cave nearly disappearing as darkness closes in.

My eyes just barely catch the movement of a shade leaping from a stalactite down onto us, faster than my mouth can open to warn Resmé.

Her face freezes as long black claws strike through her chest, forcefully snatching her from the circle.

"No!!" I yell from the deepest part of my core, attempting to lunge after her. But it's too late.

A powerful invincible force pulls me further into darkness with breathtaking speed.

As if looking through a long dark tunnel, I can just make out Resmé's body as she stretches her hand towards us, ensuring the portal is completely closed before a wave of black figures wash over her.

My cries become silent as the oxygen disappears, my lungs no longer present to take a breath. The feeling of Acia's hand is gone, as is the feeling of my body and limbs. The terrifying sensation of nothingness overwhelms me completely, my own fearful thoughts echoing through the darkness.

"Yes child, let your fear draw you closer to us."
Hisses a chorus of voices. The same voices that reached

out to me during my first visions with Resmé.

"Stay away from me," I scream in my mind, *"Stay away from all of us."*

Sinister waves of laughter ripple through the darkness in response, slowly fading into silence once again.

Light suddenly appears in the distance—red, glowing, and fast approaching.

Realizing that my body is present once again, I feel a heat against my skin that is quickly becoming more intense. The pulsing red light ahead now resembles a cluster of stars and gas columns similar to those I've seen in astronomy books, seemingly stretching for miles before fading into empty space.

As I enter the colossal red gas clouds, I see thin threads of light weaving in between the empty space. They form a spiraling web that leads to the pulsating red center miles ahead. As a thread of light passes through my arm, I feel as though a white-hot blade has been pressed deep into my skin, muscle and bone. I've never felt a pain so pure, even from Seth's own hand.

I'm grateful that I'm unable to hear my own screams, especially as more threads pass through my chest, stomach, and legs. The force pulls me faster through this tortuous web, my body feeling as though it's being ripped apart by ragged shards of scorching hot glass. Before my consciousness fades, the pulsing red glow completely envelopes me as I reach the enormous spherical center. A rush of hot, humid air brushes against my skin before blackness closes in around my eyes.

CHAPTER SIXTEEN

The distant sound of Acia's voice slowly pulls me into consciousness. As I force my eyes to open, her blurred face hovers over mine, and flakes of snow fall directly onto my eyelashes.

"Snow?" I murmur.

"Thank goodness," Acia says tearfully, pulling me into an embrace. "You were so still; I didn't think you would wake up."

Despite my relief at seeing her, excruciating pain courses through me as she moves me slightly from my place on the hard ground.

"I'm so glad you're okay," I say with a wince. "I've never felt something like that before. Do you know what happened?"

My entire body feels as though I've been hit by a truck, or multiple. I'm shocked that my bones aren't broken as I examine my arms and legs.

"Resmé must've not been able to sustain the bridge when she-" Acia's hands clasp over her face, her shoulders shaking as she begins to sob.

"They killed her Ethan. We were so close, and they killed her." Her fists strike the ground repeatedly and she begins to hyperventilate.

I gather my strength and pull her into an embrace.

"We don't know that, she could have escaped the moment we lost sight of her. We have to keep hope right now." Despite the steadiness in my voice, I feel tears welling up in my own eyes as the memory of Resmé's body flashes across my eyes. *There has to be hope. There must be.*

Acia softly places her fist on my chest, tear filled eyes looking around us.

"We're alone, completely alone. We separated from Quinn and Felicia somehow, I don't know where we are."

Finally adjusting my eyes, I scan our surroundings. We're inside a deep valley, miles of tall dead grass stretching off into the horizon over the hilly terrain in front of us. It appears to be sunset, although I haven't seen sunlight this brilliant red before. The blood-like color spreads across the sky and through the dark swirling clouds.

"-you think we're somewhere on Earth?" I ask, closely observing the familiar trees and plants around us, their branches completely bare.

Acia's eyes narrow as she looks over the rocky hills.

"Something's off here. It's familiar, but…not."

I gaze up into the dark clouds, placing my hand out to catch one of the flakes. Instead of melting against my palm, it leaves a gray powdery stain.

"Ash." I say quietly, grinding it between my fingers. "But where is it coming from?"

Acia nods towards the hills. "Whatever's on the other side of there. I'm not too eager to find out." She reaches down to help me to my feet.

The excruciating pain of pins and needles shoot through my legs, forcing me to lean on her for a moment.

"Why does it seem like you're handling this a lot better than I am." I ask with a halfhearted laugh.

"I've traveled with Resmé and Horace dozens of times, skin's gotten a bit thicker after a while I suppose."

She supports a bit of my weight as we pace towards the hillside, each step becoming a bit easier as my body recovers. From the corner of my eye, I see the strap of Resmé's leather satchel protruding from the grass several feet away from us.

Acia stoops to pick it up. "She went back for this; it must be something important."

She unlocks the buckle, lifting out a heavy brown book. Its cover looks incredibly ancient with countless symbols etched into the material, a single red jewel decorating the center. She traces her fingers along the edges, attempting to pull the pages open.

"It won't budge" she says, her knuckles turning white as she pulls a bit harder.

"I've seen this in Resmé's study before, but I don't have any idea of what could be inside. Hopefully there's something in it that can help us." She frustratingly places the book into the satchel before slinging my arm around her shoulder.

We continue our ascent up the hillside, taking several pauses as my legs are still regaining strength. I notice how strikingly silent the air is, not a single bird, car or plane. Just hot, sticky wind weaving in between the dead grass around us.

"When did he turn on us." Acia breathes heavily, the pain in her voice cutting through the silence like a razor.

"How didn't I sense it, how didn't Resmé, how didn't you…"

I'm hesitant on how to answer her. I'd mistaken the darkness inside Seth for a mere bullying tendency, or even jealousy. I couldn't have imagined how bloodthirsty he truly felt inside. In hindsight, his lack of empathy and aggression becomes strikingly obvious. With the complexity of this attack, he must've been devising this plan for quite a while. *But how could his intentions be covered for so long?*

The answer suddenly seems obvious.

"His illusion abilities." I say, struggling to maintain a steady breath as we near the top of the hill.

"He could've shielded his true thoughts behind a projection. It makes it easier that neither of you would suspect him."

Acia is silent for a moment as realization falls over her. She stops walking, covering her face again with her torn gray sleeves.

"What if Horace is still back there, tranced like I was, or dead-". Her voice quivers as she unsteadily wipes away tears.

"This is all just so wrong; we were never meant to separate. None of this is going to work if we're separate."

I hold her hand tightly, drawing her tear-filled eyes into my own.
"We're here together, we're alive. If we're going to figure any of this out, we're going to have to hold on to hope. Just stay here with me, please."

Another tear falls before she nods, gripping my hand tighter as we near the top of the slope.

Both of us gasp in astonishment as the other side comes into view.

"Houses." Acia mutters in bewilderment, our faces frozen as we realize the vastness of this place. Stretching in all directions and beyond the horizon are houses. White, identically built brick houses aligned perfectly equidistant from each other.

Their black rooftops create the effect of a vast dark ocean reaching further than our eyes can see. Streams of thick black smoke flow from every chimney, swirling into the sky and raining down as ash.
There's not a single person, animal, vehicle or blade of grass in sight. Not a movement, no sounds. The gloomy red sky above creates a hellish landscape, reminiscent of something from my nightmares.

"What is this place?" I whisper to myself, my heart slowly sinking into my stomach.

A deeply nefarious energy saturates the air, sending a wave of chills across my entire body. Each breath feels heavy, weighted with an eerie foreboding that hangs in the atmosphere like a thick fog.

Acia's cold hand closes around mine tightly as we stand on the edge of the steep ridge, feeling isolated and powerless as the immenseness of this mysterious world closes in around us.

This is a place of evil, a place of darkness.

Thank You for Reading!
Scan For Series Updates & More

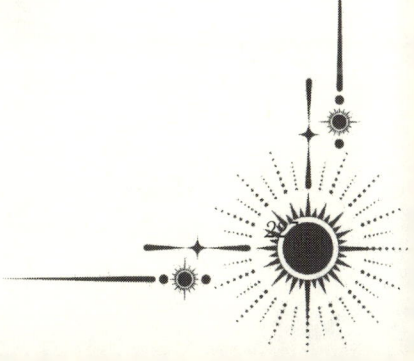

Made in the USA
Middletown, DE
07 February 2024

48655189R00135